MAGIC OF THE BAOBAB

MAGIC
OF THE BAOBAB

BY

YVONNE WHITTAL

MILLS & BOON LIMITED
ETON HOUSE 18–24 PARADISE ROAD
RICHMOND SURREY TW9 1SR

First published in Great Britain 1978
by Mills & Boon Limited

© Yvonne Whittal 1978

Australian copyright 1978
Philippine copyright 1991
This edition 1991

ISBN 0 263 77312 4

Set in Linotype Plantin 10 on 11 pt.
97-9108

Made and printed in Great Britain

CHAPTER ONE

A TRICKLE of perspiration made its way down the hollow of Olivia's back as she locked the entrance to the small shop and stepped back to admire the painted sign above the door. Logan's Bookshop & Stationers. It looked good, she decided, gently massaging the back of her aching neck and grimacing at the dampness of her skin. She had worked long hours during the past week in order to open up for business on the first day of September, and D-Day was at hand.

This was bushveld country in the northern Transvaal, where the winters were warm, and the summers wiltingly hot. The shop, as well as the small flat above, was air-conditioned, and Olivia knew that, in the height of the summer, she would not regret the money spent on having it installed. The previous owner had moved further south to a cooler climate when his hardware business had failed to prosper, and lack of sufficient funds had prevented him from having the very necessary air-conditioning installed, so Oom Hennie and Tante Maria Delport from the general dealers next door had informed Olivia soon after her arrival.

'He was alone, and getting on in years,' Oom Hennie Delport had explained. 'When one is younger one can take the heat, but it eats away at your stamina when you're older like Tante Maria and myself.'

Olivia could well believe this, for the late afternoon sun on that last day in August seemed to scorch her through the thin cotton blouse, stinging her bare arms and legs as she walked towards the entrance of the shop beside her own in search of the coolness its interior had to offer.

Oom Hennie Delport's thin, bony frame straightened

5

behind the counter as Olivia stepped across the threshold. 'So you're ready to open up for business tomorrow?'

'As ready as I'll ever be,' Olivia sighed, the corners of her soft mouth lifting as she lowered herself on to the high stool and rested her elbows on the counter. 'My flat is still in a mess, but I'll just have to sort that out in my spare time.'

Tante Maria, grey-haired, plump and motherly, came in from the small storeroom adjoining their shop and took one look at Olivia's tired, shiny face before she exclaimed, 'What you need, my girl, is a strong cup of tea after the way you've been slaving away all day.'

'Tante Maria, you spoil me,' Olivia protested, finding no difficulty in using the courtesy titles of uncle and aunt, which is a custom among the Afrikaans-speaking people.

'You need spoiling,' the older woman insisted, her keen glance raking Olivia's small, slender frame from head to foot. 'You look as though a breeze could knock you over.'

She disappeared into the small kitchen at the back without another word, and Olivia turned to face a smiling Oom Hennie as he said: 'You're in danger of being fattened up, *kindjie*. Where she has failed with me,' he gestured, drawing Olivia's attention to his own thin body, 'she is determined to succeed with you.'

A quick smile flashed across her elfin-shaped face. 'You've both been very good to me since my arrival two weeks ago, and I can't tell you how much I've appreciated it.'

Hennie Delport shook his grey head. 'Except for the odd one here and there, you'll find the residents of Louisville are all very friendly and helpful.'

'You have a large farming community, I believe,' Olivia remarked with interest. 'Are they all cattle ranchers?'

'This is cattle country, *kindjie*,' Oom Hennie reminded her. 'If you really want to see some splendid Afrikaner stud cattle, then you should go out to Mountain View some time.'

'Mountain View?'

'It's the biggest cattle ranch in the district,' Tante Maria chipped in, placing the tray of tea on the counter and busying herself with the pouring as she spoke. 'Mountain View belongs to Bernard King, and he is appropriately called the Cattle King in these parts.'

'He is the wealthiest farmer in the district,' Oom Hennie added as their tea was placed in front of them, and a plate of home-made biscuits handed round. 'His sister is married to one of our local doctors, Dr O'Brien, and you can be sure you'll meet her some time in the future. We have our annual Show in January, and Vivien O'Brien is one of the organisers. Everybody has to become involved.'

They discussed the coming Show at great length before Olivia returned to her flat above the shop and stood for a moment staring about her tiredly. Except for several crates which stood about waiting to be unpacked, and the kitchen curtains which still had to be hung, the place was almost habitable, but it would have to wait a little longer, for she had promised herself an early night after the final hectic preparations in the shop.

In the bathroom she stripped quickly and stepped under the shower, welcoming the coolness of the water on her skin as she washed her short auburn hair and soaped her body. She hummed softly to herself, excited about this new venture, and silently thanking her Aunt Georgina for the unexpected legacy which had made it all possible.

Wrapping a thin robe about her body a few minutes later, she went through to the kitchen to prepare herself something to eat, but she paused a moment in front of the window, staring down into her small, cemented courtyard where a flamboyant tree stood in the one corner, spreading out its branches like an umbrella offering shade. It was only just beginning to sprout new young leaves, and soon the garden bench and table beneath it would be shaded completely from the penetrating rays of the Transvaal sun.

Beyond the high wall lay Oom Hennie and Tante Maria's large back garden with its fruit trees and vegetable patches. Their shop was on a corner stand, and their home directly behind it for the sake of convenience. Their flower garden was a pleasurable sight, Olivia had found when she had paid them a visit over the week-end, and Tante Maria had insisted that Olivia should come round whenever she wished to pick fresh flowers to place on the counter in her bookshop. Olivia had accepted her generous offer rather hesitantly but, knowing them a little better now, she knew that they would feel deeply hurt if she did not make use of their offer.

A gentle smile curved her lips as she turned away from the window. There was still plenty to do before she could call herself settled in, but she was determined to enjoy every moment of this new life she had made for herself.

As Oom Hennie had predicted, Vivien O'Brien arrived at the shop during the first week to introduce herself, and Olivia found her an unpretentious woman in her early thirties, with dark hair combed back and twisted into a chignon of sorts in the nape of her neck. Elegantly dressed in an expensive floral silk creation, she surveyed Olivia in her pale blue, serviceable cotton frock and smiled, the dark eyes beneath the curved brows displaying a warm sincerity that banished Olivia's initial nervousness at meeting the sister of the obviously much revered Cattle King.

'It's about time someone opened up a bookshop and stationers in Louisville, and I can't tell you how thrilled I am about it, Olivia,' she remarked with an easy familiarity.

'I'm glad you think so, Mrs O'Brien.'

'Vivien,' she corrected firmly. 'Here in Louisville we're all like one big family.'

'I must say I've found everyone extremely generous and helpful,' Olivia acknowledged.

'I wonder if you could help *me*, Olivia,' Vivien smiled,

fingering the arrangement of anemones on the counter. 'I would like to purchase a book on flower arrangements.'

'Did you have anything specific in mind?'

'Not really,' Vivien laughed with some embarrassment. 'But I would prefer something which isn't too difficult to follow.'

'I think I have exactly what you require,' Olivia informed her as she went across to the shelves and returned with an impressive-looking book. 'It explains the art of flower arranging step by step from the elementary right through to the advanced stages.'

Vivien, relying entirely on Olivia's judgment, said instantly, 'I'll take it.'

'But you haven't even looked at it,' Olivia protested, slightly taken aback.

'I don't have to,' came the prompt reply. 'Judging from this arrangement,' she gestured towards the anemones, 'you obviously know what you're talking about.'

Olivia coloured slightly and looked away. 'Was there anything else?'

'Yes,' Vivien nodded, glancing about her. 'I would like to buy a book for my niece who's at boarding school here in town. She has a passion for adventure stories and I thought I could take it along for her.'

'You'll know her preferences better than I do, so would you like to select one yourself?'

'May I?'

'Certainly,' Olivia assured her, directing her to the shelf where the children's books were on display.

When Vivien had finally made her choice, Olivia wrapped the two books separately while Vivien glanced about her appreciatively once more.

'Frances will simply love your shop,' she told Olivia quite frankly. 'Being an only child she spends hours reading whatever she can lay her hands on, poor darling.'

'Being an only child can be a very lonely existence,'

Olivia agreed quietly, recalling her own childhood spent with her spinster aunt.

Vivien O'Brien glanced at her curiously, but Olivia, reluctant to discuss her personal life with a comparative stranger, remained silent, and Vivien did not pursue the subject.

'You must come and have tea with me one Saturday afternoon when you're free,' she offered pleasantly.

Olivia thanked her politely for the invitation, but as she watched Vivien leave she shrank from the idea. 'Know your place and don't venture beyond it,' her Aunt Georgina had always said, and Olivia, shy and withdrawn, had never found any difficulty in obeying that command. Now, at the age of twenty-six, with her shyness overcome to a certain extent, she was still inclined to be withdrawn, preferring to retire in the evenings with a favourite book instead of mixing with her friends and their families. Granted, her circle of friends had never been large and once they were all married she found, to her dismay, that they had nothing in common any longer. The result was that, after her aunt's death, she had found herself completely alone, and it was then that she had realised how wrong it had been of her to shrink away from close relationships. Opening up this shop in Louisville was part of the personal therapy. She had to meet people and learn to mix, but Vivien O'Brien was something quite different, and the invitation could only have been uttered out of politeness, Olivia told herself.

Later that afternoon as she walked towards the door to close up the shop for the night, a red sports car drew up against the kerb and a young man jumped from the front seat without bothering to open the door.

'Am I too late?' he asked anxiously, and Olivia stepped back, indicating that he should enter.

'A few seconds longer wouldn't matter.'

He hastily selected a few notebooks and pencils, returning swiftly to the counter in order to pay for them. 'I'm

Gerald Thatcher,' he introduced himself. 'And you are?'

'Olivia Logan,' she replied, glancing at him with interest. 'Are you also a farmer?'

'Good heavens, no,' he laughed humorously. 'I'm the vice-principal of the local school. Do I look like a farmer?'

'No,' she admitted reflectively, her glance taking in his lean, tanned fairness and the impeccable grey suit. 'I'm finding it rather difficult to judge by appearances. I have always thought of farmers as people with sunburnt features, but here in Louisville that description applies to almost everyone.'

'In this climate you acquire a tan even while you're in the shade,' he informed her gravely as they stepped out on to the pavement. 'Could I offer you a lift home?'

She suppressed a smile with difficulty. 'You wouldn't have far to go, because I live above the shop.'

'Oh,' he said, sounding a little perturbed as he glanced up at the flat before meeting her direct gaze once more. 'Will I be seeing you again?'

'If the service in my shop was to your satisfaction, Mr Thatcher, then I certainly hope we shall see each other again,' she prevaricated, misunderstanding him deliberately.

'My name is Gerald,' he persisted with a display of determination, 'and I meant would you allow me to take you out somewhere one evening.'

'I——' She hesitated, biting back the natural instinct to refuse. 'We don't know each other at all, Gerald, but if your offer is a genuine one, then I think I would like to go out with you one evening.'

'I'll telephone you,' he promised, his green eyes smiling into hers before he jumped into his car and started the engine. '*Tot siens*, Olivia.'

'Gerald Thatcher,' Olivia began hesitantly the following morning when Tante Maria arrived with freshly baked scones for her tea. 'Do you know him?'

'He's a very nice boy,' she replied without hesitation. 'He's only been here since the beginning of the year, but he has already become such a valued part of the community that it feels as though he's been here much longer.' Tante Maria's blue eyes twinkled mischievously. 'Do you fancy him?'

'Well, I only met him very briefly yesterday,' Olivia admitted blushingly.

'And you're going to see him again?' she guessed shrewdly.

'Well ... yes,' Olivia admitted reluctantly, lowering her glance to the pencil she twisted so mercilessly between her agitated fingers.

'I'm glad,' Tante Maria announced. 'It's time you stopped hiding yourself away in that flat of yours. A young, attractive girl like yourself should have plenty of young men queueing up for dates.'

Young and attractive, Tante Maria had called her, Olivia thought as she stared at herself in the mirror that evening. Young, yes ... but attractive? No! Her large grey eyes were set too wide apart, her nose was too small, and her mouth too wide. There was nothing one could call attractive about her features, she decided critically, but she was totally unaware of the captivating length of her thick, dark lashes which so often veiled her expressive eyes, and the tender curve of lips suggesting a vulnerability that would no doubt awaken the protective instincts in the opposite sex. Small and slender, with her silky auburn hair cut short to curl softly about her face, she looked much younger than her twenty-six years, and it was no wonder that Oom Hennie, as well as several other people in Louisville, called her *kindjie*. Child.

Since coming to Louisville she had felt more like a child than ever before; a trusting and innocent child trying to make a living for herself in the world of adults.

Sighing heavily, she climbed into bed and tried to read, but her thoughts interfered with the words on the printed page until she finally gave up the effort and switched off the light.

Olivia received an unexpected visitor one afternoon during the following week. An extremely pretty child, with her dark hair braided into two neat plaits that hung down her back, entered the shop, and Olivia allowed her to browse about, but she finally looked up from the tapestry she was struggling with when she became aware of dark eyes studying her intently from across the counter.

'Are you Olivia Logan?'

'That's right,' Olivia smiled, lowering her tapestry to study the small, perfect features. She was not one of the children who called regularly at the shop, and Olivia felt certain that she would have remembered her had she seen her before.

'My Aunty Viv told me about you.'

'Oh?'

'I'm Frances King,' the child enlightened her almost accusingly.

'Oh,' Olivia repeated foolishly, realising at last that this was Bernard King's daughter, and the niece Vivien O'Brien had spoken of. 'If I remember correctly, then your Aunty Vivien told me you were at boarding school. Are you allowed out of the hostel grounds whenever you wish?'

'Of course not!' the child said indignantly. 'Our study period isn't for another hour yet, so I thought I'd slip away to have a look at your bookshop.'

'Do you enjoy reading, Frances?'

'Oh, yes. Very much,' came the enthusiastic reply.

'How old are you?'

'Ten,' Frances replied, her manner much older than her years as she settled herself on the high stool and leaned with her elbows on the counter. 'How old are *you*?'

'I'm twenty-six,' Olivia replied without hesitation, and with equal honesty.

'You don't look that old,' Frances remarked after a thoughtful pause, her dark eyes observing Olivia closely. 'Why did you come here to Louisville?'

'I travelled through here once and liked what I saw,' said Olivia, somewhat startled by her direct question.

'My daddy says that people who come to a small place like this, after living in the city most of their lives, are usually running away from something they can't face.'

Olivia smiled inwardly. 'Your father obviously has strong ideas on the subject.'

'*Were* you running away from something?'

'You could say, I suppose, that I was running away from the loneliness,' Olivia replied slowly as she met the child's direct gaze. 'One can become very lonely in a city like Johannesburg where everyone rushes about in their own private little world with no time to stop and say "Hello".'

'Were you lonely?' Frances wanted to know with some urgency. 'Were you really lonely?'

'Yes, I was,' Olivia admitted, realising for the first time with startling clarity just how lonely she had been after her aunt had died, and it was with the money Aunt Georgina had left her that she had bought this small bookshop in an effort to escape that loneliness. She became aware of a flicker of sympathy in the dark eyes appraising her, and asked, 'Are you lonely sometimes?'

'Sometimes,' Frances admitted.

'But you must have lots of friends at school.'

'I suppose so,' Frances agreed sullenly. 'But they want to play such stupid games at times that I think I prefer being alone with my books.'

Olivia suppressed a smile as she asked, 'Do you have lots of books to read?'

'Oh, yes.' Her expression cleared miraculously. 'Daddy sometimes buys me something special when he flies to

Johannesburg on business, and Aunty Viv is always bringing me books to read.'

'Your Aunty Vivien must be very fond of you,' Olivia observed seriously.

'Daddy says she spoils and fusses me too much, and that's why I'm at boarding school and not living with Aunty Viv and Uncle Peter,' Frances explained with complete honesty. 'They haven't any children of their own, you know. Daddy says Aunty Viv can't have any.'

'I didn't know that,' Olivia replied, feeling strangely sympathetic towards a woman she had met only once, but Vivien O'Brien was not a woman one forgot easily.

'Are you married?' Frances asked suddenly as the silence lengthened between them.

'No.'

'Have you got a boy-friend?' Frances persisted with intense curiosity.

'No,' Olivia laughed, glancing at the electric clock against the wall. 'Frances . . .' she hesitated, biting her lip. 'I enjoy talking to you, but if you're not supposed to be here . . .'

'No one will miss me,' Frances insisted confidently.

'Someone just might,' Olivia insisted gently. 'Can you imagine how worried your daddy and mommy would be if someone at the hostel telephoned them to say you were missing?'

'There's only my daddy,' Frances informed her a little carelessly. 'My mommy died when I was four.'

'Oh.' Olivia felt like kicking herself. After a few weeks in Louisville she still knew very little about the people in the town and surrounding district. 'I'm sorry,' she added a trifle inadequately.

'May I come again?' Frances asked eagerly, changing the subject.

Olivia nodded. 'If you promise to get permisson from the Matron at the hostel first.'

'All right,' Frances agreed readily. 'I'll come again soon.'

Olivia stared after her until she was out of sight, wondering what exactly it was about this child that interested her so much that she was already looking forward to her next visit. Could it be Frances King's apparent lack of shyness, or the hint of loneliness which she had been allowed to glimpse only briefly? Whatever it was, Olivia decided eventually, Frances was an arresting and amusing child, who obviously thought the world of her father, and did not care who knew it.

When Gerald Thatcher telephoned later that afternoon inviting Olivia to have dinner with him at the Haskins Motel, she accepted eagerly in the hope of finding out more about her young visitor, but Gerald, she discovered that evening as they faced each other across the candlelit table, was more interested in discussing her personally.

'How long have you been here in Louisville?' he asked as they sipped their wine in the Motel restaurant with its potted palms and glittering silverware.

'Approximately three weeks,' she replied after a swift calculation.

He shook his head in disbelief. 'Why has it taken so long for me to meet you?'

'Perhaps because you only came into my shop for the first time the other day,' she reminded him with a humorous smile.

'Hm ...' he nodded, his fair hair gleaming in the subdued light. 'We have been rather busy lately,' he explained thoughtfully. 'We're trying to get the children involved in making something for the annual Show in January.'

'It's quite an event then, this Show?' Olivia questioned seriously.

'Absolutely,' Gerald confirmed, his glance questioning. 'Are you entering anything?'

'Oh, no,' she laughed with a touch of embarrassment. 'I'm not at all artistic in any way.'

Gerald's green eyes mirrored disbelief, but the waiter

arrived with the menu and for a time they had to discontinue their conversation.

'Tell me about yourself,' Gerald urged once the waiter had retreated with their order, and his green glance lingered on the creamy curve of her shoulders.

'There's nothing much to tell,' she protested, colouring slightly. 'I've led a very ordinary, nondescript life which makes boring conversation.'

'Let me be the judge of that,' he insisted, and Olivia smiled resignedly.

'Well, I was at university in Johannesburg for a few years and eventually qualified as a librarian, which isn't a very unusual or exciting job, but I enjoyed it.'

'What made you come to a small place like this?'

Olivia pulled a face, wishing she had a cent for every time that question had been put to her. 'Oh, I ... had a little money that was just aching to be used and, when I drove through here a few months ago and noticed that there was a shop for sale with a convenient flat above it, I decided to buy it.'

'Just like that,' Gerald mocked her deliberately casual reply.

'Well, not quite like that,' she admitted laughingly. 'I went home and thought about it for a while before deciding finally.'

'Then all I can say is, Johannesburg's loss is Louisville's gain.'

'You're very kind,' she passed off his remark, but his hand found hers across the table with a confidence which could only have resulted from experience, she was certain.

'It's the truth,' he insisted.

Olivia slipped her hand from beneath his and curled her fingers about the stem of her glass. 'It's your turn to tell me about yourself.'

His green eyes laughed into hers, but he obliged nevertheless. 'After leaving the university almost seven years ago, I taught for a while in Pretoria before I accepted a transfer back to Johannesburg. Then, last year, I was offered this post here in Louisville.'

'And where do you go from here?'

'Nowhere, I hope,' he replied firmly, his glance capturing hers once more. 'Not now that I've met you.'

Olivia suppressed the laughter that bubbled up inside her as she shook her head reprovingly. 'Gerald, how many girls do you have dangling on a string to whom you've said those exact words?'

'None, I swear,' he protested convincingly.

'None?'

'Well, maybe a few,' he admitted finally with an embarrassed laugh, his eyes crinkling humorously at the corners.

'Shame on you!' she rebuked him with a smile.

'You know, Olivia,' he said, regarding her thoughtfully after a moment, 'I think that's what I like about you. You certainly cut me down to size.'

'I'm sorry,' she said with a measure of regret.

'Don't be sorry, Olivia,' he insisted with a look of determination on his lean face. 'You've merely challenged me to work much harder at convincing you that I'm serious.'

His remark disturbed her considerably, making her withdraw mentally from him. 'Gerald, I don't think——'

'I know,' he interrupted abruptly. 'We're practically strangers, and you're not the kind to fall in love at first sight, but that doesn't mean that we can't spend some time together getting to know each other, does it?'

'No, I suppose not,' she agreed after a moment of thought.

'There you are, then,' he smiled with satisfaction.

'Gerald, do you know Frances King?' she asked, changing the subject after they were served with shrimp cocktails.

'Bernard King's daughter?' he asked with a measure of

surprise, and she nodded briefly. 'I see her almost every day, but I wouldn't say that I know her. Why?'

Olivia sampled her starter before replying. 'She came to the shop this afternoon.'

Gerald's eyebrows rose sharply. 'You mean she left the hostel grounds?'

'Yes.'

'The Matron will have something to say about *that*,' he frowned severely.

'Gerald, promise me you won't say anything about it?' she pleaded hastily. 'Just this once, please?'

'How can I refuse when you ask so nicely?' he smiled warmly, his glance curious. 'What did the child want?'

'I think she came mainly out of curiosity because she enjoys reading, but we talked for quite some time.'

'What about?'

Olivia shrugged carelessly, reluctant to discuss the rather personal conversation she had had with the child. 'Nothing that would interest you, Gerald.'

He leaned towards her in the secluded intimacy of their corner table and captured her glance with his. 'Everything you say and do interests me, Olivia.'

'Gerald, please,' she whispered, lowering her lashes.

'All right,' he laughed softly, applying himself to the cocktail before him. 'Why are you so interested in the child?'

'I don't know,' she admitted thoughtfully. 'There was just something about her that made me curious to know her better.'

'If you want to know more about Frances King, then you should talk to Sanet Pretorius. She's her class teacher.'

'Sanet Pretorius?' Olivia repeated slowly, a frown creasing her brow. 'I'm sure I've met her, but I can't recall what she looks like.'

'She's a pretty little thing with fair hair and big brown eyes,' he elaborated promptly, and Olivia's glance sparkled with unaccustomed humour once more.

'Do you know her well?'

His face creased into a smile. 'I've taken her out a couple of times, but she's far too serious for me.'

'Serious in what way?' she probed, enjoying his discomfiture.

'Let's say she took *me* too seriously.'

Olivia regarded him intently for a moment before she said: 'I'm beginning to think you're a coward about becoming seriously involved with a woman.'

'What do you mean?' he demanded instantly.

'I think——' she hesitated abruptly, shaking her head and wishing she had not allowed her tongue to run away with her in the first place.

'Come on,' he insisted good-humouredly. 'You made a statement, now clarify it.'

'Well ...' she began hesitantly before plunging into the rest of her speech. 'You're attractive, charming and attentive; three qualities which, I'm sure, most women would find irresistible, and I think you may consciously, or unconsciously, encourage them to fall in love with you, but the moment they commit themselves, you retreat smartly.'

He studied her for a moment in silence, and the low murmur of voices in the restaurant seemed to increase with her nervousness before he said uncomfortably, 'You're making me squirm.'

'Am I right?'

'Yes ... and no,' he admitted with a rueful smile. 'I don't deliberately encourage them to fall in love with me and, if I do retreat, then it's because I feel I'm not ready for marriage yet.'

'Do you intend adding my name to that list?' she asked wryly.

'No, Olivia,' he shook his head slowly. 'I realise you're far too astute to be fooled by someone like myself.'

CHAPTER TWO

OLIVIA awoke to find the early morning sunlight streaming into her bedroom through the open, gauzed window. Even at this early hour of the day the heat could be felt, she thought, flinging back the bedclothes as she smothered a yawn and stretched lazily, a smile curving her lips as she recalled the evening spent in the company of Gerald Thatcher. She had found him a relaxing and amusing escort, but she had swiftly labelled him, 'Not to be taken seriously'.

After a splendid dinner, punctuated with lighthearted conversation, he had driven her home and, realising that his usually irresistible charm had awakened nothing more than feelings of friendship, he had not endeavoured to do more than drop a light kiss on her cheek as he said goodnight. Olivia had to admit to herself that she liked him, and that she would regret losing his friendship one day, but she knew without doubt that friendship was all there would ever be between Gerald and herself.

A casual glance at the alarm clock on the bedside table halted her thoughts and sent her hurrying through to the bathroom, admonishing herself for lying in bed so late when there was still so much to do before the shop had to be opened that morning but, despite her late start, Olivia unlocked the door to the bookshop at precisely eight-thirty, and stepped inside. She seldom had customers this early in the mornings, but it would create a bad impression if someone were to arrive unexpectedly and find it closed, she realised as she sighed and went through to the back to switch on the kettle in order to make herself a cup of instant coffee.

Waking up later than usual that morning had left her no time for the usual leisurely cup of coffee, and neither had there been time to collect fresh flowers from Tante Maria's lovely garden, she realised now as she glanced ruefully at the wilting daffodils on the counter. She would have to get rid of them before someone walked in, she decided, collecting her wandering thoughts sharply as the kettle boiled, sending up a cloud of steam.

Apart from several familiar faces, Vivien O'Brien was the first person to enter her shop later that morning whom Olivia knew by name. She purchased a few magazines and asked politely after Olivia's health until her interested glance rested on the tapestry Olivia had pushed aside the moment she had entered.

'How absolutely beautiful,' she remarked excitedly as she held it up to examine the floral design which was nearing completion. 'I'm working on a landscape scene for the Show, and you simply must enter this as well.'

'Oh no, I couldn't,' Olivia protested hastily, quaking inwardly at the mere thought of displaying her meagre attempt at something she knew really very little of.

'Why not?' Dark brown eyes mirrored astonishment. 'Everyone must enter something, and you've done some marvellous work on it, Olivia.'

'I don't usually go in for tapestries, but this was given to me by my aunt before—before she died,' she explained haltingly. 'I haven't any paintings on my walls up in the flat, and that's why I'm in rather a hurry to finish this so that I can have it framed.'

'I'll give you the name of an excellent place in Johannesburg,' said Vivien, taking a last look at the tapestry before returning it to its original place on the counter and, scribbling down the name and address of the firm she had mentioned, she added, 'Everyone here sends their tapestries to this firm for framing, but you really should enter it in the Show, you know, Olivia.'

Olivia recoiled almost physically from the idea. 'I'd never dream of entering my poor effort! It would be most embarrassing to have people laughing and whispering behind my back at my obvious audacity.'

'Nonsense!' Vivien said sharply. 'When I drop in next time I shall bring my tapestry along with me, then you can see for yourself that there's nothing fantastic about my entry. I'm not an expert at such crafts, either, but I make them and enter them in the Show mainly for the fun of participating.'

Olivia lowered her glance uncomfortably. 'Perhaps, but I still don't think——'

'There's still plenty of time, so think about it,' Vivien interrupted persuasively, picking up her magazines and saying she must hurry home.

Olivia stared after her retreating figure until she was out of sight, then, lifting her tapestry to examine it more closely, she shook her head firmly. Vivien was merely being kind, she decided. Her tapestry was good enough only to adorn the empty wall in her flat above, and she was not going to let Vivien persuade her otherwise.

With the latest magazines arriving just before her lunch hour, Olivia found herself being kept fairly busy that afternoon until she found a slender, fair-haired young woman facing her across the counter. The face was familiar, and the large brown eyes made her wonder.

'You know, I'm having an awful time trying to put names to faces,' she said conversationally in an effort to qualify her suspicions. 'We've met before, but . . .'

'I'm Sanet Pretorius,' the girl introduced herself with a quick, friendly smile.

'Oh, yes,' Olivia replied, her brow clearing as she recalled the information Gerald had given her the previous evening. Here was her opportunity to find out more about Frances King, but she would have to take care how she went about it, or people might begin to wonder, as they were bound to do in a small place such as Louisville. 'I met one of your class pupils the other day. She told me her name was Frances King.'

'She's quite an interesting child. Very adult for her years, and very clever,' Sanet smiled thoughtfully, passing on a fragment of information before Olivia had had the need to enquire.

'Such behaviour can usually be attributed to children who've grown up mainly among adults,' she remarked with care, for some reason reluctant to make it known that she knew considerably more about the circumstances involving the child.

'I'm certain that this is the reason for Frances' behaviour,' Sanet admitted, needing little encouragement to continue with her observations. 'She's been at boarding school since the age of six, but I'm afraid she doesn't mix very well with the other children.'

Gerald Thatcher walked into the shop at that moment, forcing them to discontinue their discussion and, after greeting them in his usual cheery fashion, he gave Sanet Pretorius the full benefit of his irresistible green glance.

'If I'd known you were coming to town I would have given you a lift.'

Olivia, observing them unobtrusively, saw a quick flush stain Sanet's cheeks while her dark eyes lit up as if someone had put a match to a candle. She saw, too, a flicker of tenderness in Gerald's eyes; a tenderness she was almost certain he was unaware of.

'That's very kind of you, Gerald, but I enjoyed the walk,' Sanet replied, a breathless quality in her voice as she edged towards the door, and a tremor in the hands that gripped the magazine so tightly. 'Well, I must be on my way home again. Goodbye, Miss Logan——' She hesitated, her glance returning to the fair-haired man like a moth attracted to the light before she added, 'Cheerio, Gerald.'

'Just a moment,' Olivia said quickly, her sympathetic

heart dictating her actions as she prevented Sanet's departure and turned to face Gerald. 'Was there anything else you wanted to do in town this afternoon? I mean after you left here?'

Gerald frowned slightly. 'Well ... no ...'

'Then why don't you offer Miss Pretorius a lift home?' she prodded him gently in what she hoped was the right direction.

Sanet's eyes widened with alarm. 'That really isn't necessary. I don't mind the walk, and——'

'But of course I'll give you a lift home, Sanet,' Gerald interrupted firmly, fired into action, much to Olivia's delight. 'It would be silly not to, considering that we're both going in the same direction,' he continued, his persuasive charm having the desired effect on Sanet as she hovered in the doorway. 'If you'll just give me a few seconds to get a tablet of drawing paper, then I'll be right with you.'

'Well, if you're sure ...'

'Naturally, I'm sure,' Gerald insisted, his brilliant smile conquering Sanet completely while Olivia, feeling ridiculously like Cupid, made a pretence of being completely oblivious of the emotional little scene she had just witnessed.

Sanet Pretorius *had* taken Gerald seriously, she realised after they had gone. But it was much more than that, if her inexperienced observations had been correct. Sanet was in love with Gerald. The flushed cheeks, the trembling hands, and the breathless quality in her voice had told Olivia that more clearly than words could have done. And Gerald? Was it possible that, despite his protestations to the contrary, he was more than mildly interested in the young teacher he had once taken out a few times? If he had had no interest in her at all, would he have agreed to her suggestion so readily that he should offer Sanet a lift home?

'Oh, dear,' she said to herself with a measure of concern.

'I hope I haven't interfered in something which could only bring that girl further unhappiness.'

'Hello! Is anyone here?' a child's voice brought Olivia hurrying from the back of the shop.

'Frances!' she exclaimed softly, her glance going with swift pleasure over the child's sturdy frame dressed in a floral cotton frock and sandals before she met the dark eyes focussed so intently on her person. 'I was wondering when I would see you again, but I'm so glad you decided to come today because Tante Maria has sent me a date loaf to have with my tea, and I couldn't possibly eat it all by myself.'

'Tante Maria makes the best date loaf in the district,' Frances informed Olivia as she followed her into the back where she was making tea and slicing the date loaf under discussion. 'Did you know that?'

'No, but I can believe that because everything else she makes is absolutely delicious,' Olivia admitted, thankful for the flask of iced orange juice she had brought down after lunch as she poured it into a glass for Frances before she poured herself a cup of tea.

'Miss Logan ...' Frances began hesitantly once they had returned inside and sat facing each other across the counter.

Olivia smiled encouragingly at her. 'When you call me Miss Logan, you make me feel ancient, so what about calling me Olivia?'

'Daddy says it's disrespectful for children to call adults by their first names.'

Bernard King obviously took an interest in his child's upbringing, Olivia realised, impressed by the child's remark. 'If I give you permission to call me by my name, then that makes a difference, doesn't it?'

'I suppose it does,' Frances admitted at length, making instant use of this new freedom as she asked, 'Olivia, may I sit behind the counter with you?'

'Of course you may,' she agreed instantly. 'Can you

bring that stool round to this side by yourself?'

'It's not very heavy,' Frances replied, testing its weight before carrying it round to Olivia's side.

'There you are,' Olivia smiled, placing the glass of orange juice in front of Frances and shifting the plate to within easy reach. 'Now, let's eat that date loaf. I'm dying to taste it!'

The slices disappeared one after the other, indicating that Frances was either hungry, or possessed an exceptionally good appetite. Whatever the reason, they soon emptied the plate between them.

'Do you like books?' Frances wanted to know, her dark eyes questioning above the rim of her glass.

'I enjoy reading them,' Olivia admitted, glancing about her at the shelves filled with reading matter to suit all tastes. 'I also love holding a beautifully bound book in my hands, and feeling the quality of the paper between my fingers. Books have their own particular smell, did you know that? Whether it's the paper, the ink, or the material used for binding, I wouldn't know, but I think I could be led blindfolded into a library and I would know where I was.'

'Did you have a bookshop in Johannesburg as well?'

'No,' Olivia shook her head, focussing her attention on Frances once more. 'I worked in a library.'

Dark eyes lit up with interest. 'Were there millions of books in the library?'

'Well, not quite as many as that,' Olivia smiled, steering the conversation away from herself. 'What are you going to do when you leave school one day?'

Frances frowned, drawing her brows into a straight line. 'I wanted to become a cattle rancher like my daddy, but Daddy says farming isn't for women, and I should rather take a degree in something more suitable.'

'Oh,' Olivia said inadequately. It was not unusual for women to take up farming these days, but, if Bernard King had other ideals for his daughter, it was none of her business. 'Have you decided yet in which direction you would like to study?'

'No,' Frances replied, draining her glass and placing it on the counter. 'Not yet.'

'You still have plenty of time to decide, though,' Olivia reminded her gently, wondering suddenly what Frances' serious little face would look like when it was creased with laughter.

'That's what Daddy says too.'

Judging by her expression this was a painful subject to Frances, and Olivia changed the direction of the conversation yet again. 'Do you go home every week-end, Frances?'

'Yes,' the child responded, her expression becoming quite animated. 'Daddy fetches me on a Friday afternoon, and brings me back on a Monday morning. I hate Monday mornings,' she said fiercely. 'Especially after a nice weekend.'

'You enjoy your week-ends at home, then?' Olivia prompted casually.

Frances slipped her hands beneath her thighs and swung her legs to and fro on the high stool, her reminiscent glance going beyond Olivia. 'When Daddy isn't too busy we take the horses and ride into the veld. There's a big baobab tree on Mountain View, and we sometimes have a picnic lunch there because it's so close to the dam if we want to have a swim.' Her intelligent glance met Olivia's. Did you know that the stem of a baobab tree can be anything up to twenty-eight metres in circumference?'

Startled by the child's extensive vocabulary, Olivia said: 'No, I didn't know. I've never seen a baobab tree close up, only from a distance while travelling in my car.'

'Why don't you come out to Mountain View this weekend, then I could show it to you,' Frances offered eagerly. 'We've got plenty of baobab trees on our farm besides that big one which is very old.'

Olivia's mind ticked over rapidly in order to decline the

invitation in a way that would not hurt Frances' feelings.
'It's very kind of you to offer, Frances,' she managed
eventually, 'but I don't think your father will take kindly to
having a stranger like myself arriving on his doorstep. Not
even for the purpose of admiring the baobab trees on his
ranch.'

'Ilona Haskins is always there and Daddy doesn't seem
to mind,' Frances scowled, making her displeasure clearly
evident.

'She's a friend of your father's, and that makes a difference,' Olivia reasoned carefully.

'I'll just tell Daddy that you're *my* friend.'

Olivia stared at her for a moment, a peculiar warmth en-
casing her heart. 'Am I your friend, Frances?'

'Yes,' came the adamant reply, the determination in the
small jutting chin matching the expression in her dark eyes.
'I like you. You're not like Ilona Haskins, and I wish ...'
Heart-shaped lips were drawn into a thin line. 'I wish
Daddy would tell her to stay away from Mountain View.'

'If your father enjoys Miss Haskins' company, then you
must try to accept her presence there,' Olivia replied with
gentle firmness, not wishing to encourage Frances' apparent
dislike, but Frances would not be swayed.

'I don't like her, and she doesn't like me either.'

Olivia's eyebrows rose in shocked surprise. 'How can
you be so sure?'

'I can tell by the way she looks at me when Daddy's not
there to see,' Frances replied without hesitation, leaving
Olivia speechless with the realisation that, if Frances was
speaking the truth, Bernard King was having the wool
pulled thoroughly over his eyes. Frances herself broke the
tense silence by glancing regretfully at the clock against the
wall. 'I'd better go now.'

'Thank you for coming, Frances,' Olivia said, gathering
her wits about her with an effort. 'And take care on the way
back to the hostel.'

'I will, and ... Frances slid off the stool and hesitated,

her glance suddenly pleading. 'Olivia, promise you'll come out to Mountain View some time?'

An unaccustomed tightness gripped Olivia's throat. 'I can't promise, but I'll try ... some time.'

Satisfied, Frances sped from the shop, leaving Olivia with several disturbing thoughts racing through her mind. Was Frances correct in her assumption concerning Ilona Haskins, or was she merely rejecting the possibility of someone taking her mother's place in the future? Children have been known to become jealously possessive of their one remaining parent, and Frances, so intense at times, could quite easily fit into that category.

Olivia cleared away her supper dishes that evening and went round to Oom Hennie and Tante Maria as she had promised earlier that day and, as they sat around the scrubbed wooden table in Tante Maria's spacious kitchen, the conversation inevitably turned to her young visitor that afternoon.

'I saw Frances King at your shop again this afternoon,' Tante Maria broached the subject, her curious glance meeting Olivia's briefly while she poured the coffee.

'Between the two of us we practically finshed the date loaf you brought me,' Olivia admitted, smiling as she recalled Frances's absorption until the last crumb had been cleared from the plate. 'It was delicious. Thank you.'

'That child's lonely,' Oom Hennie muttered, filling the bowl of his pipe with tobacco and striking a match.

'She's more than lonely,' Tante Maria added forcefully, placing their cups in front of them and lowering herself into a chair. 'She needs a mother, but I feel sorry for her if Ilona Haskins ends up being that mother.'

Olivia frowned down at the table. 'Frances doesn't appear to like her very much.'

'Very few people do like Ilona Haskins,' Tante Maria enlightened Olivia despite her husband's warning glance. 'She's very beautiful and very charming, but underneath that lovely exterior there's a hardness that's unbecoming in a woman. She wants Bernard King, and she's made it perfectly obviously by the manner in which she's hung around him since his wife died six years ago.'

Olivia was beginning to believe Frances' remarks about this woman she had yet to meet. 'Do you think Mr King will marry her eventually?'

'I can't say,' Tante Maria shrugged, 'but if he does want to marry her, then he's certainly taking his time about it.'

'Perhaps he's thinking of his daughter,' Olivia observed thoughtfully, recalling partly her conversation with Frances that afternoon. 'It sounds as though they enjoy a good, healthy relationship.'

'Bernard King idolises his daughter,' Oom Hennie chipped in, puffing happily at his pipe and filling the kitchen with the aromatic odour of his particular brand of tobacco. 'He's also very strict, I believe.'

'I only hope that, whatever he decides, he doesn't jeopardise his daughter's future happiness,' Olivia stated, feeling inexplicably protective towards a child she had only met twice.

Tante Maria's glance was curiously intent, and faintly humorous. 'It seems to me that you've developed a soft spot for Frances King.'

A soft spot! Could one call it that, this warmth that invaded her heart each time she thought of Frances? Olivia pondered this in silence until she became aware of two pairs of eyes watching her closely, and questionably.

'She's a very pretty child, and very intelligent,' she explained lamely, a faint mist clouding her vision as she added, 'And she says I'm her friend.'

Blinking rapidly to prevent the ridiculous tears from spilling over her lashes, she missed the enquiring glance that flashed between her two elderly companions, but finding nothing amiss when she eventually raised her glance and changed the subject.

Vivien paid Olivia a visit the following afternoon, bringing along her own tapestry as she had promised. She was very persuasive in her efforts to make Olivia change her mind about entering her tapestry in the Show, but Olivia managed to avoid committing herself by inviting Vivien to have tea with her and skilfully changing the subject.

Vivien was, Olivia discovered, a very lonely woman despite her involvement with the organisation of the local Show. Her husband, Peter, had his regular surgery hours twice daily, and the rest of the time he was out on call, leaving Vivien very much to herself during the days, and quite often during the nights as well.

'I'm not complaining,' Vivien assured her hastily. 'I knew what I was letting myself in for when I married a country doctor, but ...' Her expression grew wistful. 'If we could have had a child, but ...' she smiled resignedly. 'Miracles don't always happen—not to me anyway.'

Not wishing to mention the fact that Frances had already enlightened her in this respect, Olivia remained silent, but Vivien apparently did not expect a sympathetic reply to her remark, for her attention had been diverted by some or other activity outside the shop.

'That's strange,' she muttered frowningly, meeting Olivia's questioning glance. 'I just saw Bernard passing in his Land Rover, and he doesn't usually come to town in the middle of the week. I wonder if something has happened to Frances?'

Anxiety gripped Olivia. 'Do you think she might be ill?'

'I hope not,' Vivien said firmly, gathering up her tapestry bag and rising to her feet in an unconsciously graceful movement. 'I'd better go home because, if she is ill, Bernard will bring her along to the surgery.' She smiled apologetically at Olivia, but her smile was tinged with concern. 'I'm sorry I have to rush off like this, but I must be at home in case I'm needed.'

Olivia assured her hastily that she understood perfectly,

and moments later she found herself alone with her own troubled thoughts concerning Frances, wishing that she had the right to telephone the hostel to enquire after the child. In an effort to brush off her uneasiness, she took the empty cups through to the back and rinsed them under the tap in the basin.

She was fortunately kept busy for the next hour, leaving her little time to ponder the reason for Bernard King's unexpected trip to Louisville. It was really no concern of hers to be so anxious about a child she hardly knew, she told herself sternly, and yet . . . !

As the last customer left the shop, Olivia sighed tiredly, but her peace was shattered seconds later by the sound of a vehicle door being slammed with force moments before heavy footsteps entered her shop. She relinquished her task of straightening the books on the shelves and turned, her smile freezing on her lips as her glance encountered the ferocious-looking man who stood towering over her menacingly. Except for the broad forehead, straight dark brows above dark, angry eyes, high cheekbones, and aristocratic nose, the rest of his features were obscured by a black beard which was flecked abundantly with grey. A wide-brimmed hat with a leopardskin band was tilted at an arrogant angle on his equally dark head, and, as he stepped towards her, she was made aware of the smell of the sun and the veld which clung to him. Unreasonable and unaccustomed fear made her back away involuntarily, but the shelves dug into her back, halting her progress.

'Miss Logan?' he queried abruptly, the deep timbre of his voice vibrating along her nerves as she became alarmingly aware of his enormous height and broad, powerful shoulders which tapered down to slim hips.

'Yes?'

'Bernard King,' he enlightened her harshly, at the same time answering her silent, frantic query as to the familiarity in the shape of his eyebrows and the intensity of his dark brown eyes fringed with thick black lashes. It was almost impossible to believe that this enormous man, clad in khaki bush jacket and pants that clung almost too tightly to broad shoulders and muscular thighs, was Frances' father, and something warned her that the reason for his visit was not a social one. 'I would like to know exactly what you think you're doing by encouraging my daughter to leave the hostel grounds on two occasions during the past two weeks, and offering her refreshments as enticement to repeat the offence.'

His attack was as unexpected as his appearance, and she stared at him speechlessly for a few seconds before finding her voice. 'Mr. King, I assure you, I——'

'You are aware, I suppose, that she's at boarding school, and that there are certain disciplinary rules that have to be adhered to in such an establishment?'

'I realise that, Mr. King, but——'

'You realise this, and yet you deliberately encouraged her to break one of the most important rules of the hostel?' he interrupted her in a thundering, incredulous voice that made her flinch inwardly. 'Really, Miss Logan, have you no sense at all, or does your behaviour stem from a lack of discipline in your own life?'

'How dare you!' Olivia demanded hoarsely, her anger giving her the courage to stand up to him.

'I dare, Miss Logan, because this matter concerns me as much as the hostel Matron into whose care I've placed my child while she's at school, and I can tell you now that I shall not tolerate your disrupting influence on Frances.'

'Disrupting influence!' Olivia choked out the words, unable to believe her ears and clenching her trembling hands at her sides until her nails dug into the soft palms. 'Really, Mr King, you have no right to insult me in this way! You don't know me at all, and——'

'I don't want to know you either,' he announced with ruthless disregard for her feelings as his narrowed glance slid contemptuously down the length of her, giving her the sensation that her body had been licked by scorching flames. 'You're an alien in our community, bringing with you your city habits, and I don't intend that you should influence my daughter in any way.'

Humiliation sent the blood rushing to her pale cheeks as she fought to control the trembling of her limbs. 'Those are harsh words, Mr King.'

'They're nothing compared to what might occur if Frances sets foot in this shop again,' he threatened, emphasising his remark, and his height, by taking a further step towards her, and making her cringe inwardly from him when she almost felt the anger vibrating through his large frame.

'Does this mean that you've—you've forbidden her to come here again?' she asked through stiff, unwilling lips as she lowered her anguished glance to the tanned column of his strong throat, and lower still to where the dark hair on his chest was clearly visible above the opening of his bush jacket.

'Not only have I forbidden her to come here again,' he elaborated, a tanned, powerful arm making a sweeping gesture to indicate the interior of her shop, 'but I've forbidden her to communicate with you in any way.'

The colour receded from her cheeks at the finality in his voice. 'I . . . see.'

'I'm glad you do, because there's to be no misunderstanding in future,' he ground out the words, his dark eyes boring into hers as if he wished to burn every single word into her very soul. 'Good day, Miss Logan.'

He touched his hat briefly and strode from the shop while Olivia, shattered by their encounter, watched in almost hypnotised fashion as he climbed into his dusty Land Rover, slammed the door, and drove away at speed. Only then did she realise that she had been supporting her trembling body by clutching at the shelves behind her and,

walking jerkily across to the nearest stool, she subsided on
to it and closed her eyes to shut out the vision of the most
insufferable man she had ever met.

She had realised instantly, of course, that Frances had
not done as she had suggested, and that her visit the previous afternoon had once again been without permission.
Unable to defend herself because of her reluctance to make
matters worse for Frances, she had had to swallow Bernard
King's insults, but the painful remarks still had the power
to make her wince as she sat there fighting to regain composure.

He was the devil himself, she thought, every detail of his
appearance imprinted indelibly on her memory. Perhaps
it was the awe-inspiring size of the man and the ferocious-
looking beard that made him so frightening, while those
dark eyes, almost black with anger and dislike, had sliced
through her composure like a hot knife through butter.

'Poor Frances,' she murmured softly, and yet she recalled how the child's expression had lit up each time she
had mentioned her father. Perhaps, in a different mood,
Bernard King might not appear so fearsome, but she was
not likely to have the opportunity to find out—not after
all the insults he had flung at her that afternoon.

Well, she had met the Cattle King at last, and the meeting had certainly left an impression on her, an impression
that did not fail to make her pulse quicken with alarm, as
well as increase her dislike each time she thought of him.
In a small town such as Louisville they would undoubtedly
meet again, but on the next occasion she would be
armoured against his forceful personality, and imposing
appearance. There was no likelihood either that they would
move in the same circles, for Bernard King's friends would
be far too exalted for someone like herself; an alien with
detestable city habits.

CHAPTER THREE

BERNARD KING'S stormy visit, accompanied by his stinging accusations, had left Olivia feeling unsettled and rest-
less. The week-end did little to alleviate her concern for
Frances, and what the child might have had to endure because of her misdemeanour, but, after forbidding her to
come to the shop again, he would surely not punish Frances
further, would he?

Olivia pressed her fingers against her eyes as she sought
to obliterate the image of the man she had heard so much
about, and whom, after their unfortunate encounter, she
disliked so intensely.

'I shan't tolerate your disrupting influence on Frances,'
his cutting remarks returned to haunt her. 'You're an alien
in our community, bringing with you your city habits.'

An alien, indeed! Oh, God, what did he think she was?
His words had stung, making her an outcast, and painfully
aware of the loneliness she had wanted so desperately to
escape from by making her home in Louisville. Was that
how most people saw her? As an alien who had to be
tolerated, but not always befriended?

The chime of the doorbell made her fight back the heed-
less tears as she went to answer it. Gerald stood on the
doorstep, the smile on his lean face almost sending her flying into his arms in a flurry of relief. She could not remember when last she had been so happy to see anyone as
she was to see Gerald on that uneventful Sunday afternoon.

'I know it's rather hot, but I thought a drive into the
country would have its compensations,' he suggested,

mopping his brow as he stepped past her into the coolness of her lounge.

'Just give me a moment,' she smiled before hastening to her room to touch up her make-up, and to check on the the appearance of her cool, cream-coloured dress that clung so softly to her slender figure. Satisfied, she pulled a comb through her hair and went through to the lounge.

'Am I mistaken in thinking you were glad to see me?' Gerald asked with a hint of a smile on his face as his small red car shot away from the kerb.

'As a matter of fact, I was suffering from a bout of self-pity,' she laughed self-consciously, enjoying the feel of the breeze whipping against her cheeks as a result of the hood being left down. 'Your friendly face has made all the difference,' she added, shaking off her mood partially.

His hand touched hers briefly where it lay on the seat beside her. 'I'm happy to know I came at just the right moment.'

He drove several kilometres out of Louisville to a road-house where they sat beneath the cool shade of a mopani tree and ordered iced fruit drinks.

'Would you like to talk about it?' he suggested, noticing the slight downward curve of her lips, and Olivia, after initially rejecting the thought of confiding in Gerald, found it a relief to speak of her meeting with Bernard King.

'It wasn't funny,' she accused as Gerald, after listening intently, burst out laughing.

'You shouldn't take it so seriously,' he explained, controlling himself. 'I know the man looks awesome with that beard of his, but he's not entirely as bad as you imagine. He had a right to be angry, you must admit, and you could clear up the misunderstanding without much difficulty if you wanted to.'

'Not without involving Frances,' she argued promptly, 'and I have no interest whatsoever in seeing Bernard King again.'

'Louisville is a small place,' Gerald reminded her with a humorous grin. 'You're bound to meet again.'

'I'm sure the town is big enough for Bernard King and myself to live quite comfortably without having to cross each other's paths too often,' she stated adamantly, but her heart wept at the thought of not seeing Frances again. 'It amazes me to think that such a hateful man could have such a charming sister, and such a delightful child.'

Gerald made no comment, but Olivia, feeling decidedly better after talking to him, relaxed and enjoyed the scenery as they drove back to town. Louisville, lying at the foot of the range of mountains with its high peaks, appeared deceptively peaceful that Sunday afternoon, but after the quiet, lazy weekdays, the town became a hive of activity on a Saturday morning. Everyone in the district came in to Louisville to do their weekly shopping, and it was on such days that Olivia often wished she had an assistant.

'By the way,' Gerald remarked drily as he stood beside her on the pavement outside her shop some time later, 'that was a clever bit of manipulation the other day when Sanet and I were in your shop.'

'You don't mind, do you?' she asked, glancing at him unobtrusively. 'You seemed quite keen once I'd suggested you gave her a lift.'

'Oh, I didn't mind at all, but I had hoped to have a little more time with you,' he replied, his green glance narrowed against the sun.

'She's very pretty, isn't she?'

'Very pretty,' he admitted, glancing away down the quiet street.

'You're very fond of her.'

'Yes—no! What is this?' he demanded with an embarrassed laugh as he turned to face her. 'Have you set yourself up as Cupid, or something?'

'I wouldn't dream of playing Cupid,' Olivia protested, crossing her fingers hopefully behind her back. 'I was merely curious as to how you felt about her, and you *are* fond of her, aren't you?'

Gerald's face reddened slightly. 'Yes, I am fond of her, but I can't afford to become serious about any girl at the moment.'

'Why not?' Olivia demanded, having wormed such a mighty confession out of him.

Gerald lowered his glance and kicked self-consciously at a pebble on the pavement with the point of his shoe. 'Sanet's parents are very wealthy, and my salary wouldn't be nearly enough to—to——'

'To support her in the way to which she's accustomed?' she finished for him, understanding so much more now than she had before when she saw him nod his head in confirmation. 'Then marriage *did* cross your mind where Sanet is concerned,' she stated confidently, watching the colour surge into his cheeks once more.

'It did, but——'

'And you never told her?' she interrupted softly, beginning to wilt in the heat of the sun, but determined to get to the bottom of the problem.

'How could I?' Gerald demanded.

'Do you think it's fair to let her go on thinking you don't care, when in fact you do?'

His green glance met hers with complete candour. 'It's better not to commit oneself when you find yourself out of your depth, and Sanet, lovely as she is, will get along just fine without me around to create problems.'

'I'm not so sure,' Olivia murmured, but Gerald was already getting into his car and waving goodbye.

Olivia awoke the following morning almost before the first rays of the sun had touched the tips of the mountain peaks, and she welcomed the fact that it was Monday morning, the beginning of another week after the inactivity of the weekend. She was kept reasonably busy that morning, but went through a slack period that afternoon which gave her the opportunity to check up on her orders. It was almost with a sigh of relief, though, that she looked up to see Vivien entering the shop in order to purchase her weekly magazines.

'I believe you've suffered Ufezela's poisonous sting,' she remarked with some amusement, her dark eyes observing Olivia closely as she paid for her magazines.

'Ufezela?' Olivia queried hesitantly, her eyes widening.

'The scorpion,' Vivien explained, making herself comfortable on the stool beside the counter. 'Bernard acted as farm manager on a cattle farm in Natal a number of years ago, and the Zulus there gave him the name Ufezela. The name has remained with him ever since.'

Olivia was not at all surprised at the name given to him, for she had indeed felt the sting of the scorpion, and it still caused her considerable discomfort. 'Did your brother tell you about—about coming here and—and——'

'Yes, he told me,' Vivien interrupted her halting query. 'But don't take too much notice, my dear. His anger usually subsides as quickly as it flares up.'

'Did Frances tell you anything?'

'She never mentioned the subject, but speaking of Frances,' Vivien added, her expression sobering instantly, 'she's not at school today. She's been running a fever all week-end, and Peter can't seem to find the cause. There's nothing organically wrong with her, but the fever is persisting, and Peter says that if it doesn't subside within the next two days, he's going to suggest Bernard fly her to a specialist in Johannesburg.'

'She's at home, then?' Olivia asked with swift concern.

'Oh, yes,' Vivien smiled. 'Bernard has insisted that she stay in bed until the fever passes.' A glint of humour sparkled in her eyes; eyes that were almost as dark as her brother's. 'He's a very doting father, despite his other shortcomings.'

A doting father he might be, Olivia thought after Vivien

had gone, but that was still no reason for him to insult her in the way he had done, and it was something she would *never* forgive him.

She slept badly that night because of her growing concern for Frances and, after a night of tossing and turning, she felt utterly listless the following day. She waited expectantly all day for Vivien to drop in with some news about Frances, but there was no sign of her as the time moved steadily onwards to five o'clock that afternoon. She was on the verge of telephoning Vivien at her home when the telephone in the shop rang shrilly. She lifted the receiver eagerly, but the blood drained from her face as she heard that now familiar voice say:

'Is that you, Miss Logan?'

'Yes, Mr King,' she replied, keeping her voice cool despite the anxiety that seemed to knot her stomach.

'My sister is on her way to you at this moment to drive you out here to Mountain View,' he said without preamble, and Olivia almost dropped the receiver in her agitation.

'But, Mr King, I——'

'Vivien will explain when she gets there,' he interrupted with harsh impatience and, before she could say another word, the line went dead.

How dared he treat her this way! Olivia fumed as she slammed the receiver into place. He had a nerve to think she would set foot in his home after the insults she had had to endure. Nothing on earth would induce her to go out to Mountain View, she decided angrily, dismissing the matter promptly from her mind.

Vivien took one look at her furious expression when she entered the shop just before closing time, and said: 'I gather Bernard telephoned you?'

'Yes, he did,' Olivia admitted, raising her chin defiantly. 'But you might as well know that I have no intention of going out to his home with you.'

'Not even for Frances' sake?' Vivien countered, a satisfied little smile playing about her lips as she noticed Olivia's altered expression. 'She's asking for you, and Peter suggested that it might have the desired effect on her health if you went out and saw her.'

'Frances wants to see me?' Olivia demanded a little breathlessly, her anger and reluctance evaporating almost instantly in the face of this information.

'She's been asking to see you all week-end, but she's become quite frantic about it now, I believe,' Vivien replied calmly, and Olivia's concern for Frances swept aside all the firm decisions she had made about never setting foot on Mountain View.

'In that case I shan't be a moment,' she told Vivien, diving behind the counter for her bunch of keys and checking that everything was in order before she locked up for the night.

'Frances is an extremely lonely child,' Vivien remarked conversationally as they sped through the town in her small blue Fiat and headed north. 'It's such a pity that Aileen wasn't able to have another child.'

'Aileen?' Olivia questioned curiously, glancing at the elegantly dressed woman beside her and wishing that she had had time to change into something more appropriate for her visit to the Cattle King's ranch. But what the devil did it matter how she looked? she admonished herself sharply. He most probably would not even notice her, and neither did she care one iota whether he would be there or not.

'Aileen was Bernard's wife,' Vivien's explanation cut across Olivia's thoughts. 'She died tragically six years ago in a car accident when Frances was four.'

Olivia accepted this information in silence, curious to know more about the woman who had been married to Bernard King, yet not inclined to make her curiosity known to Vivien.

Mountain View, appropriately named for its breath-

taking view of the magnificent mountain range just beyond
Louisville, was situated ten kilometres out of town. It was
a vast piece of land, Olivia discovered, dense with trees and
rich in soil. They drove through several sturdy iron gates
before they came to the stone-pillared gateway leading up
to the sprawling, thatch-roofed homestead, with its gauzed-
in verandah running along the front and west side of the
house. Under the jacaranda tree with its clusters of purple
flowers stood a bottle-green Triumph, and Olivia jumped
nervously as Vivien exclaimed:

'Oh, drat! That woman is here again.'

'I beg your pardon?'

'Ilona Haskins,' Vivien enlarged, a frown settling between her brows as she gestured vaguely towards the Triumph. 'Somehow she's always here whenever I come out to
Mountain View.'

Olivia smiled slightly at her irritability as she stepped
gingerly from the car and, while waiting for Vivien to join
her, she allowed her appreciative glance to take in the
scarlet poinsettias and bougainvillaea which lent a brilliant
splash of colour to the spacious garden with its lawns and
various varieties of shady trees.

'This way,' said Vivien, touching her arm, and Olivia's
limbs were set in motion with some reluctance.

On the wide verandah they were met by the bearded
monster, as Olivia had began to think of Bernard King, and
beside him stood a tall, slender woman with the most flaw-
less skin Olivia had ever seen on a redhead. The green silk
creation clinging gently to her curvaceous body spoke of
wealth, the colour matching her eyes to perfection as they
now appraised Olivia with cool speculation while the in-
troductions were being made, and Olivia was never certain
afterwards which she had found most disturbing—Ilona
Haskins' slightly contemptuous glance as she took in
Olivia's pale lemon cotton frock which had seen the best of
two summers, or Bernard King's dark piercing glance,

slashing her quite mercilessly with his evident dislike.

'So you're the one Frances has been so anxious to see,' Ilona's silky voice penetrated the uneasy silence. Beautiful and poised, her lips twisted a little cynically as she gazed up at the man beside her. 'Doesn't it make you wonder, Bernard, what this is all about?'

'I have a pretty good idea,' his deep voice set Olivia's nerves quivering as he gestured to the glass of amber liquid in his large hand. 'Could I offer you something to drink, Miss Logan?'

'No, thank you, Mr King,' she declined, the coolness of her own voice surprising her while she trembled inwardly with nervous haste to accomplish the reason for her visit.

His gaze flickered insultingly down the length of her before coming to rest on his sister who had stood silently beside Olivia with a faintly amused expression on her face. 'And you, Vivien?'

'Iced lime juice will do nicely, thank you,' she smiled up at her brother, an easy familiarity and warmth in her manner as she linked her arm through Olivia's. 'But I think I'll take Olivia through to Frances first. She's bound to have heard us arrive.'

Bernard King inclined his head slightly and stepped aside. 'As you wish.'

With Vivien leading the way, Olivia found herself in a spacious entrance hall, the stark black and white tiled floor lending a further coolness to the interior, but her glance was irrevocably drawn towards the old-fashioned half-moon table against the wall on to which a broad-brimmed hat had been dropped carelessly, the leopardskin band denoting the ferocity and strength of its owner. Three rooms led off the entrance hall. One, Olivia could see, was the living-room, but the two remaining doors were closed, and she guessed them to be the dining-room, and quite probably a study.

There were two passages ahead of them, one leading straight ahead and the other turning off to the left. Vivien took the latter, and moments later Olivia found herself standing just outside the door of Frances' room.

Vivien touched Olivia's arm, holding her back a moment longer as she said softly, 'I won't be able to stay long, so I'll drive you back to town as soon as you've spoken to Frances, if that's all right with you.'

Olivia nodded silently, and Vivien retreated, leaving her to enter Frances' room alone. The brass door-handle was cool against her fingers as she turned it and opened the door slowly.

'May I come in?' she asked softly, glimpsing a spacious, airy room beyond, with a patch of late afternoon sunlight on the carpeted floor.

'Olivia!' she heard Frances exclaim a little hoarsely and, pushing the door open further, she stepped into the room to find the child in bed, propped up against the pillows on the old-fashioned copper bed, her cheeks flushed, and her dark eyes shimmering with a suggestion of tears. Her fingers clutched agitatedly at the sheet as she stared at Olivia. 'I was afraid you might not come after—after what happened.'

Olivia left the door slightly ajar as she approached the bed and sat down on the edge where Frances had made room for her, her throat tightening at the unnecessary anxiety in the child's eyes. 'How could I stay away when I knew you wanted to see me?'

'I had to see you,' Frances insisted, clearly agitated as she fidgeted in bed. 'I'm glad they let me see you alone.'

'I didn't know you were ill, Frances, until your Aunty Vivien came and told me yesterday,' Olivia explained, suspecting the reason for Frances' agitation. 'What's the trouble?'

'Oh, nothing much ...' Frances' voice trailed off into a momentary silence before she added off-handedly, 'I've got a fever.'

'I can feel that,' Olivia smiled, raising one of her hands

to touch Frances' brow. 'You're so hot you're burning my fingers.'

A strained silence hovered between them before Olivia felt the small hands gripping her fingers tightly. 'Olivia, I had to see you.'

'Had to, Frances?' Olivia asked, unaware of the tenderness in her grey glance which had a comforting effect on the child.

'To say I'm sorry about what happened,' Frances enlightened her, a frown creasing her feverish brow. 'It was all my fault.'

'I did tell you to get permission from the Matron before coming to the shop again,' Olivia reminded her gently.

'I know.' Frances lowered her glance, biting her lips nervously before confessing, 'I knew the Matron wouldn't let me go if I asked her, so I just ...'

'You just slipped away again,' Olivia filled in for her understandingly when her voice trailed off into silence.

'Yes, I ...' Frances looked up, but her glance shifted to beyond Olivia, her dark eyes widening with unmistakable alarm. 'Daddy, I ...'

Olivia glanced swiftly over her shoulder, a similar feeling of alarm coursing through her veins at the tall, broad-shouldered figure dwarfing the large doorway. He approached the other side of the bed slowly, his hands thrust deep into the pockets of his khaki pants, and Olivia's heart hammered heavily against her ribs as she met his dark, probing glance. How much of their conversation had he heard? she wondered frantically, searching for something to say to relieve the unbearable tension in the room as she once again felt Frances' hands tightening on her fingers until the nails bit into her flesh.

'It seems I owe you an apology, Miss Logan,' he said at length, his deep voice travelling like shock waves along her nervous system. 'It is Frances who was at fault, after all.'

So he *had* heard, she realised, drawing a quick, nervous

breath as she passed the tip of her tongue across her dry lips. 'Please, Mr King, I can explain.'

'I'm sure you can, but why didn't you explain this to me when I confronted you in your shop?' he demanded with characteristic harshness, his dark eyes offering her no leniency.

'You never gave me much opportunity, and I——' she swallowed nervously, 'I didn't think it was necessary to make matters worse for Frances.'

'I see,' he said after another long, drawn-out silence had been overcome during which Olivia had wished frantically for escape; escape for herself as well as the poor shivering Frances.

'Are you angry with me, Daddy?' she heard Frances ask timidly, and her heart contracted instantly with a warmth and sympathy she had never experienced before.

'Very angry,' he confessed unsparingly. 'I said some very nasty things to Miss Logan which were entirely unnecessary, and I hope you've apologised as well.'

'That's why I wanted to see Olivia,' Frances replied, her glance directed pleadingly at her father.

'Who gave you permission to use Miss Logan's name?'

'I gave her permission, Mr King,' Olivia intervened swiftly, challenging him to deny her the right to make such a request from his daughter, but he gave her nothing more than a cursory glance which made her realise only too well that the truth had not diminished his dislike.

His opinion of her apparently remained the same, just as her opinion of him, despite his apology, remained the same. His insults had struck too deep to be forgotten lightly, and her usually forgiving nature would never extend as far as this bearded monster, with his dark, greying hair falling so untidily across his forehead.

'Daddy ...' Frances began tentatively. 'I *am* sorry, I really am.'

'I believe you.'

Frances, as well as Olivia, glanced up at him swiftly at the change in his attitude, and Olivia found it almost impossible to credit him with the tenderness she thought she had heard in his deep voice.

'You're not angry with me any more?' Frances demanded, her expression lightening considerably as she gazed up at her father.

'When you've done something wrong and you're genuinely sorry about it, then it's not for me to remain angry with you, is it?' he told her firmly, glancing at Olivia suddenly as if he were about to say something more, but he was interrupted by the sound of a silky voice and hasty footsteps which brought Ilona Haskins to his side.

'Bernard, my dear, I wondered what had happened to you,' she said poutingly, sliding her arm through his with a certain familiarity and an air of unmistakable possessiveness while her cool green glance settled on Olivia. 'He's mine!' those eyes warned Olivia quite clearly, and so unnecessarily.

'We were having a little discussion, but I think we've said all there is to say,' Bernard King replied, making no effort to move away from the curvaceous body pressed so close to his side as he glanced intently at Olivia. 'Not so, Miss Logan?'

'That's quite right,' said Olivia, rising hastily to her feet with the distinct feeling that she was being dismissed. 'I must go, Frances. I think your aunt wants to get back to town before dark.'

'Stay and have supper with me,' Frances pleaded, her obvious reluctance to see Olivia leave warming the uncomfortable chill about Olivia's heart. 'Please, Olivia?'

'I'm afraid I can't, I——'

'Daddy will drive you back to town,' Frances stated confidently, and Olivia became embarrassingly aware of a flush staining her cheeks as Frances turned eagerly towards her silent father. 'Won't you, Daddy?'

'Really, Frances,' Ilona intervened with a hint of irritation in her voice as her cold glance swept over Olivia's small, slender figure hovering uncertainly beside the bed. 'Perhaps Miss Logan doesn't wish to stay.'

'How tactful,' Olivia thought with secret amusement, knowing perfectly well that Ilona was in a hurry to see the back of her.

'You *do* want to stay, don't you, Olivia?' Frances persisted, contradicting Ilona's statement fiercely.

'Another time, perhaps,' Olivia replied lamely, relief flooding her being as Vivien appeared in the doorway, offering escape from this awkward situation.

'Are you ready to go, Olivia?'

'Yes, I am.'

'Olivia . . .' Her hand was clutched anxiously, detaining her a moment longer. 'Will you come again?'

A feeling of helplessness overwhelmed her as she stared down into Frances' anxiously enquiring eyes, but it was Bernard King who settled the matter abruptly.

'Naturally Miss Logan will come here again. Now get some rest, or you'll be too tired to eat your supper.'

'All right,' Frances sighed, relinquishing her hold on Olivia's hand, and sinking back against the pillows.

'I hope you get better soon, Frances,' Olivia said hastily before everyone lost their patience.

'I will, now that I've seen you,' Frances replied confidently and, quite impulsively, Olivia leaned over her and dropped a light kiss on her hot forehead.

Ilona remained in the room with Frances while Bernard walked out to the car with Vivien and Olivia. Unexpectedly, he extended a large hand towards Olivia and, after a brief hesitation, she placed her hand in his, watching it disappear almost completely within his warm, rough clasp.

'I appreciate your coming out to see Frances, Miss Logan,' he said with an amiability that sat oddly upon him as he released her hand, and she was surprised at the tingling sensation that shot up her arm.

'It's always a pleasure to see Frances, Mr King,' she replied with a coolness she was somehow beginning to reserve for this man alone.

'Drive carefully, Vivien,' he said once they had climbed into the Fiat, lowering himself from his great height in order to meet his sister's glance through the open window.

'I always do,' Vivien assured him, giving his cheek an affectionate pat before turning the key in the ignition and shifting the gear lever into position.

'What did you think of her?' Vivien demanded after Olivia had climbed back into the car after closing the final gate that marked the boundary of Bernard King's ranch.

'She was very feverish, but otherwise quite bright,' Olivia replied, settling herself more comfortably in her seat.

'I wasn't talking about Frances,' Vivien laughed shortly. 'I meant Ilona Haskins.'

'She's very beautiful,' Olivia offered, placing a guard on her tongue.

'Oh, come now.' Vivien laughed outright, keeping her eyes on the gravel road ahead. 'You can speak your mind with me, you know.'

'I don't know her well enough to risk an opinion.'

'Not even one tiny opinion?' Vivien prompted mischievously.

'Well ...' Olivia suppressed a smile, 'she appears to be very possessive.'

'Possessive, spoiled and totally the wrong wife for Bernard if he should ever think of marrying again,' Vivien elaborated all at once with a quality of steel in her manner which was very similar to her brother's. 'He needs a wife who can be firm when necessary, yet loving and gentle, and above all she must be the right mother for Frances. That child needs the loving care and companionship of a woman who'll treat her with understanding and gentleness when she reaches the age of puberty, and that isn't so many years away.'

'Perhaps Miss Haskins——'

'Ilona doesn't know the first thing about children,' Vivien interrupted fiercely. 'Ilona Haskins is of prime importance to Ilona Haskins. What she wants, she gets, and I only hope that my brother has enough sense to wake up to the fact that beauty isn't the only ingredient required in a wife.' There was a brief pause as Vivien sighed heavily. 'If only Aileen hadn't died so soon!'

Aileen! Bernard King's late wife, and the mother of his child. What was she like? Olivia wondered curiously, but she bit back the questions that rose to her lips. It was none of her business to be curious about Bernard King's personal life. The bearded monster was quite capable of taking care of himself, she decided unsympathetically.

To Olivia's disgust, her curiosity concerning Aileen King increased sharply after her discussion with Vivien and, while having coffee later that evening with Oom Hennie and Tante Maria Delport, the conversation inevitably turned once again to Bernard King and his daughter Frances. And, as usual, it was Tante Maria who left the way open for Olivia to question her further without embarrassment.

'Tell me about Aileen King,' she prompted, cupping her chin in her hands and watching a moth fluttering against the kitchen window in its pursuit towards the light.

'Aileen King was always a frail-looking girl,' Tante Maria informed Olivia while she removed a tray of ginger biscuits from the over and inserted another. 'After Frances' birth her health seemed to deteriorate, and I heard from Vivien O'Brien that the doctors had warned her against having another child. It was a terrible day when she died in that accident,' Tante Maria shook her head sadly as she lowered herself on to a chair. 'Some people said she had become neurotic about not being able to give her husband the son he desired, and that she deliberately killed herself, but that's not true. She was a well-adjusted young woman, and they were a very happy family.'

'Bernard King was a changed man after his wife's death,'

Oom Hennie remarked, sucking at his pipe in his usual thoughtful fashion. 'He became a little hard and embittered, and who can blame him entirely?'

'And Ilona Haskins?' Olivia asked after a slight pause, accepting a biscuit from Tante Maria. 'When did she appear on the scene?'

Tante Maria snorted loudly, showing her displeasure in no uncertain terms. 'Ilona Haskins swooped down on him like a vulture on its prey soon after Aileen's death, but I must also add that, if it had not been for Ilona, Bernard King would have lived a hermit's existence.'

'In what way do you mean?' Olivia asked, biting into the still warm biscuit with a thoughtful expression on her elfin-shaped face.

'Ilona Haskins isn't the kind of woman to go into seclusion,' Oom Hennie chipped in once again, his eyes twinkling with mischief. 'She's beautiful and she likes being admired, so she dragged Bernard King into the limelight with her. I must admit that, old as I am, she can make my old heart flutter.'

'Oh, she does, does she?' Tante Maria pounced on her husband in playful anger, and he made a pretence of cowering away from her, his thin shoulders shaking with laughter.

The conversation could no longer. be taken seriously after that, but Olivia had heard enough to satisfy her curiosity, illogical as it might have been.

When she entered her flat shortly after nine that evening she was startled by the sound of her telephone ringing, and she lifted the receiver a little warily to find Vivien on the line.

'I thought you might like to know that Peter has just returned with the news that Frances' fever has dropped considerably. It seems that he was right about it being a psychological thing after all, but he still insists that she remains at home for at least another day to make absolutely sure.'

'I'm so glad she's feeling better,' Olivia sighed with relief, seeing again Frances' hot, flushed face against the white pillows.

'Your presence must have had a magical effect,' Vivien laughed softly. 'What did you do?'

'Nothing really,' Olivia assured her with a touch of embarrassment. 'We merely talked a bit, that was all.'

'She's grown very fond of you in a remarkably short space of time,' Vivien observed quietly.

'The feeling is mutual, I assure you,' Olivia replied, a warmth flooding her heart.

'Well, I shan't keep you any longer,' Vivien said after a brief, reflective pause. 'I just thought I'd let you know about Frances.'

Olivia thanked her warmly and, several seconds after replacing the receiver, she remained standing beside the instrument. Was it possible that Frances had worried herself into a frantic, feverish state because of what had happened? Poor, dear Frances, who was taking their friendship so seriously, Olivia thought sadly, wondering whether she had been wise to encourage this friendship with the child.

CHAPTER FOUR

As the week drew to a close Olivia assumed that Frances had gone back to school, or Vivien would have telephoned and informed her to the contrary. Frances, it seemed, had learnt her lesson, although Olivia could not prevent herself from glancing up warily each time someone entered her shop during the afternoons, and found, to her dismay, that her relief was tinged with regret.

The Saturday dawned with the promise of being no different from any other in that week, but shortly after nine that morning it took on a new and rather startling dimension when, after returning a book to the shelf, she turned to see Bernard King and his daughter entering her shop.

'Olivia!' Frances cried excitedly, rushing towards her with bouncing pigtails to clutch at her hand. 'Olivia, could I stay here in the shop with you this morning while Daddy is busy in town? Could I, please?'

Olivia was left speechless for a moment as she glanced from Frances' anxious little face to Bernard King's bearded features. Did the man never wear anything other than those khaki clothes, heavy boots, and wide-brimmed hat? she wondered irrationally as she stammered, 'Well, I don't know, I——'

'I could help you, couldn't I?' Frances interrupted eagerly, shaking Olivia's arm as if to stress the fact that she could be useful.

'Why, yes, but——' Olivia glanced helplessly across at the man watching them in silence, his dark eyes brooding and intensely disturbing. 'Mr King?'

His name was a query on her lips that stemmed from a hesitancy to accept that he would sanction such a request

from Frances. Had he not, in this very shop, stated that
he had forbidden Frances ever to communicate with her
again? She could understand him relaxing that command
because of her illness, but she could not believe that he
would actually agree to leaving Frances with her for several
hours.

'Frances has given me no peace about bringing her to
your shop and, in order to prevent her from leaving the
hostel grounds during the week, I've agreed to bring her
to you on Saturday mornings,' he answered her unspoken
query, frowning down at her from his great height. 'If
you're certain she won't be in the way.'

'She won't be in the way at all, and I shall love having
her here every Saturday,' Olivia assured him hastily, a
great weight lifting from her heart. 'Just as long as her
being here meets with your approval.'

'You see, I told you she wouldn't mind, Daddy,' Frances
said triumphantly, glancing from one to the other.

Bernard King's eyebrows rose a fraction as he met
Olivia's direct gaze. 'I hope you realise that my apology was
sincere, Miss Logan?'

'I would like to think so, Mr. King,' she replied, feeling
a little overwhelmed, but not entirely convinced that her
opinion of him would ever change. He was the 'Bearded
Monster' as far as she was concerned, and it would always
remain so.

'I'll pick you up on my way home, Frances,' Bernard
told his daughter, in an obvious hurry now to go about his
business. 'And don't get in Miss Logan's way too much,' he
added sternly.

'I promise I won't,' Frances replied, quivering with suppressed excitement beside Olivia as her father raised his hat
politely and strode from the shop, but the moment they
were alone she turned to Olivia, seeking assurance. 'You
don't mind my coming here, do you, Olivia?'

'Darling Frances,' Olivia laughed, taking both the child's

hands in hers. 'I can't tell you how happy it makes me to have you here with me.'

'You called me "darling",' Frances observed slowly, her head tilted to one side, her glance intent. 'Does that mean you like me?'

'It means I like you very much,' Olivia admitted with grave honesty.

'I'm glad, because I like you very much too,' Frances replied instantly, flinging her arms about Olivia's waist and hugging her with surprising strength before she looked up questioningly and asked, 'Was Daddy very angry with you the other day?'

'Yes ... very.'

'*Did* he say some very nasty things to you?'

Olivia winced inwardly, but her smile was reassuring. 'Yes, but don't let it trouble you, Frances.'

'Could I help you with something?' Frances wanted to know, releasing Olivia and glancing eagerly about the shop.

'Well ...' Olivia stared about her thoughtfully. 'You could perhaps straighten the magazines on the shelves, and then you could come and sit behind the counter with me, if you like?'

Frances amazed Olivia countless times that morning. Gone was the serious-faced little girl she had known, and in her place was a laughing, happy child, with a mind eager to grasp whatever knowledge Olivia cared to impart. If some of the customers thought it strange to find Bernard King's daughter behind the counter in Olivia's bookshop, wrapping up books and helping out generally, then they merely smiled and remained silent, but Olivia knew that it would soon be a topic of conversation among the people of Louisville who knew the King family so much better than she did. Frances, however, behaved as though she belonged there, and on several occasions Olivia had to prevent herself from hugging the child profusely out of sheer delight, for the memory of Bernard King's disapproval still lurked uncomfortably in the recesses of her mind.

The 'Bearded Monster' was never far from her thoughts, and when he stalked into the shop just after eleven-thirty that morning and asked: 'Are you ready to go home, Frances?' Olivia felt herself shrinking inwardly from him as if repelled.

'Oh, no!' Frances protested instantly, her dark eyes wide and appealing as they gazed up at him. 'Please, Daddy, could I stay a little longer? Please?'

Olivia held her breath, waiting for the explosion which was sure to come, but Bernard King's deep voice sounded surprisingly calm as he said: 'Perhaps Miss Logan wouldn't mind bringing you out to the farm when she has closed the shop for the day.' Olivia's lashes flew upwards to reveal astonishment in her grey eyes as they met his brooding, enquiring glance. 'You have a car, Miss Logan?'

'Yes, I do,' she heard herself say without giving the matter much thought.

'Splendid,' he said abruptly. 'Lunch will be ready as soon as you arrive at Mountain View.'

Lunch! she thought in alarm, her heart thudding uncomfortably. 'Oh, but I couldn't——'

'Yes, yes, Olivia,' Frances chipped in excitedly. 'Stay and have lunch with us, and afterwards Daddy and I could show you our big baobab tree. Could we, Daddy?' She shot a questioning glance at her father before turning towards Olivia again with renewed confidence. 'Remember the tree I told you about, Olivia? We could pack a basket and have tea there, just as Daddy and I always do.'

Olivia felt as though she were being cleverly and methodically enmeshed in a web from which there was no escape, and, like the proverbial fly trapped by the spider, she struggled frantically for release. 'Frances, I'm afraid I can't——'

'Do you have a prior engagement for this afternoon?' Bernard King interrupted her polite refusal, his penetrating glance setting her nerves jangling.

'No, but——'

'Then the matter is settled,' he stated quite firmly and, with a paralysing numbness surging into her limbs, she watched him raise his hat and stride towards the entrance on those long, muscular legs of his. 'I'll see you both later.'

'Oh, goody!' Frances cried, bouncing up and down excitedly behind the counter, and quite unaware of the trepidation with which Olivia viewed this visit to Mountain View. 'I can't wait to show you our tree, Olivia.'

Olivia smiled weakly as she set her limbs in motion. Bernard King and his daughter were both equally overpowering when they chose to be, she decided as she endeavoured to unravel her nerves in order to get through the remained of the morning, but try as she might, she could not match Frances' enthusiasm at the prospect of spending the afternoon out at the farm. The closer it came to the time for them to leave, the more Olivia wished she had not allowed her refusal to be overruled with such ease. How on earth would she manage to get through an afternoon in the company of a man she disliked so intensely? Frances would be there, of course, but Bernard King was not someone one could ignore with ease. He made his presence felt by the mere shape and size of him, as well as the probing intensity of those dark eyes of his that seemed to miss very little.

When Olivia finally drove her Apache through town with Frances seated beside her, she discovered that she had at last accepted her fate with a calmness that was unreal and, sighing resignedly, she tried to relax the tensed muscles along her back, while at the same time loosening her frantic grip on the steering-wheel.

Bernard King seemed to appear from nowhere when she eventually parked her car beneath the shady jacaranda tree, and her legs were horribly shaky as she stepped from the car and found herself looking up into his bearded face so far above her own.

'Welcome once again to Mountain View, Miss Logan,'

he said, his manner that of a perfect host as he accompanied them on to the wide verandah. 'I thought you would both like something cold to drink before we go in to lunch,' he continued once Olivia was seated in the comfortable cane chair with Frances wriggling in beside her. 'Iced orange juice for you, Miss Logan? Or would you prefer something stronger?'

'Orange juice will do nicely, thank you.'

Olivia watched him surreptitiously as he filled three glasses from the jug which had been placed on the circular cane table, and the nerves she had struggled so valiantly to unravel become knotted once more at the pit of her stomach.

'I hope Frances didn't make a nuisance of herself?' he asked eventually after listening to Frances' excited chatter about her morning spent in the shop.

'On the contrary,' said Olivia, smiling down at the child leaning so confidently against her. 'She was very helpful, and wonderful company.'

'May I really come every Saturday, Olivia?' Frances wanted to know, seeking reassurance once again.

'I think I shall miss you terribly now if you don't,' Olivia replied with complete honesty, glancing nervously at the man relaxing in the chair opposite. 'If your father doesn't mind?'

'I have no objections,' he said abruptly, his attention claimed by the dark-skinned Venda houseboy who stepped out on to the verandah to tell them that lunch was ready. The houseboy departed as silently as he had arrived and, rising to his feet, Bernard King said: 'Perhaps, Frances, you would like to show Miss Logan the way to the bathroom so you can both freshen up before lunch, if you wish?'

Frances obeyed instantly, and Olivia, conscious of the clamminess of her hands, which she had found herself clenching so tightly on several occasions, followed her thankfully.

The dining-room, Olivia discovered some minutes later, was a cool, spacious room, furnished in teak, and with double glass doors leading out on to the verandah. Her eyes widened at the variety of cold meats and salads on the long, oval table, but she knew somehow that she would not be able to eat a thing. If it had not been for Frances, the next hour would have been the most uncomfortable in her entire life. Frances and her father ate heartily, but Olivia barely touched her food and, although her host glanced at her curiously on several occasions, he refrained from remarking upon her lack of appetite.

'Could we go and show Olivia the tree now, Daddy?' Frances asked eagerly once they had returned to the verandah.

'Yes, if you're both ready,' Bernard nodded, picking up his hat and placing it at a rakish angle on his head.

Frances' eyes glowed with excitement. 'Did you have a basket packed for us?'

'If I'm not mistaken then Evalina has it ready in the kitchen if you'd like to go and fetch it,' he smiled down at her, tugging gently at one of her pigtails. 'We'll wait outside for you.'

'I won't be long,' Frances promised, smiling up at Olivia before disappearing into the house.

'I hope you realise the extent of the influence you have over Frances,' Bernard King said stiffly as they strolled out to where he had parked his Land Rover, and Olivia was instantly on the defensive.

'I do realise it, Mr King, and I realise too how much this must displease you, considering the opinion you have of me.'

'What opinion do I have of you, Miss Logan?'

'You don't need me to enlighten you, surely,' Olivia replied without hesitation, every nerve in her body screaming out in protest as his arm brushed accidentally against hers.

They reached the Land Rover before he turned to face

her with a hint of mockery in his eyes. 'Are you such a paragon, Miss Logan, that you've never made rash statements in a moment of anger?'

'I wouldn't call personal insults rash statements, Mr King.'

'Do you want me to make you an apology in writing?'

'It doesn't very much interest me whether you do or not,' she retorted, something in his manner infuriating her. 'And I might as well make it quite clear to you that I'm here only for Frances' sake. Nothing else would have induced me to set foot in your home, or on your ranch.'

During the brief, electrifying silence that followed her statement, Olivia experienced again that flickering of fear as she had done on the first occasion they had met. What was it about this man that made her bristle like an enraged cat?

'I didn't invite you here for my pleasure either, Miss Logan,' his deep voice chilled the blood in her veins despite the heat of that October afternoon. 'You've obviously brought about a remarkable change in Frances, and for that reason only do I tolerate your presence.'

'And that puts you smartly in your place, my girl,' Olivia told herself angrily, smarting inwardly, yet knowing somehow that she had deserved it.

Frances' arrival with the basket eased the tension between them, and a few seconds later they were driving through the homestead gate and out into the veld with Olivia seated in front beside Bernard King, and Frances in the back.

The hot air fanned her cheeks and lifted her hair from her face as she looked about her with interest. She was seeing the bushveld as it actually was, lying stretched out before her in the shimmering heat of the day with the cicadas shrilling incessantly, and the wild smell of the bush permeating the air. They drove through several grazing camps which gave her the opportunity to catch a glimpse of the Afrikaner cattle Oom Hennie had mentioned. Their majestic golden-brown bodies, with the familiar hump above the shoulders and the long horns, seemed to glisten in the sunlight, their muscles rippling as they moved about among the acacia trees.

A broad-stemmed baobab tree appeared beside the track and, as Bernard King braked gently, Olivia asked, 'Is that the tree you wanted me to see, Frances?'

'Oh, no,' Frances laughed, leaning forward between their seats. 'The one we're going to show you is much bigger than that, isn't it, Daddy?'

'Very much bigger, yes,' he replied absently, glancing in the opposite direction while he kept the Land Rover moving at a slow pace. 'If you look quickly to your left, Miss Logan, you'll see a kudu bull among the trees.'

Olivia glanced in the direction he was pointing, her eyes seeking and finding the most magnificent kudu she had ever seen. Its coat was a greyish brown in colour with vertical white stripes along the sides of its body, while the long spiralled horns could quite easily have been one and a half metres long.

'It's beautiful,' she whispered, her voice tinged with regret as the kudu disappeared into the bush.

'Beautiful, but also very timid and elusive, so you're lucky to have caught a glimpse of it,' he told her imperiously, changing gear and putting his foot down on the accelerator. 'A kudu could weigh anything up to two hundred and seventy kilograms when it's fully grown,' he added.

'Do you hunt them often?'

'I hunt them only occasionally, and use their meat mostly for biltong.'

'It seems such a shame,' she sighed, shedding some of her nervousness, while her liking for biltong, those dried sticks of meat which were such a delicacy, took a definite plunge as she thought of that beautiful animal being shot.

'I don't particularly enjoy hunting down the kudu,' he said roughly, 'but when they become too many I have to diminish the herd for the sake of my cattle.'

Olivia lapsed into a thoughtful silence as the Land Rover continued to bump over the uneven track, but when they came across a second herd of cattle she could not prevent herself from saying, 'What magnificent animals! Do you breed them for slaughter, or . . .' her voice trailed off into a guilty silence as he glanced at her sharply.

'I'm mainly a stud farmer, but I do sell for the purpose of slaughter as well.' His eyes laughed at her suddenly. 'I don't keep cattle as pets, Miss Logan.'

'There it is, Olivia,' Frances exclaimed excitedly behind her, interrupting the awkward silence, and pointing straight ahead. 'Do you see the tree?'

'Yes, I do,' Olivia laughed, her own excitement mounting as Bernard King parked the Land Rover beneath the tree she had heard so much about.

'Come on, let's get out,' said Frances, opening the door and jumping to the ground without waiting for Olivia and her father.

The stem of the tree was massive and hollowed out in places. It dwarfed Bernard King so completely when he stood beside it that she had difficulty in suppressing a giggle that rose in her throat, and which finally forced her to look elsewhere. The baobab tree was comparatively short in height, but almost grotesquely fat, its oblong leaves covered in short soft hair, and its white flowers almost as large as a man's hand.

'It's enormous,' she said at last, realising that her two companions were watching her intently.

'It takes eighteen men, with their arms stretched out at their sides, to circle the stem of this tree, and it certainly makes me realise how insignificant I am.'

Bernard King could never be insignificant no matter how much he tried, she thought scathingly, but she said: 'It looks like a tree which has been planted upside down.'

'There are several legends attached to the baobab tree,' he told her casually, watching Frances clamber over the protruding roots. 'Some people believe that a very old baobab tree is eventually consumed by fire, but this story has very little substance. The tree merely disintegrates, that's all.'

'And the other legends you spoke of?' she prompted, her curiosity overcoming her uneasiness in his presence.

'Do legends interest you, Miss Logan?' His bearded face was turned towards her, the dark eyes mocking and watchful.

'They fascinate me,' she admitted, sustaining his glance and disliking him more with every second as the suspicion grew that he found her amusing for some reason.

'Tell her the one about the crocodile, Daddy,' Frances insisted, dropping to the ground and running to Olivia's side.

'Well, it's said that a draught of water in which the seeds have been soaked for some time will offer protection against being attacked by a crocodile,' he obliged, and Olivia could once again have sworn that he was laughing at her behind that ferocious beard of his. 'It's also said that a lion will devour anyone who picks one of the flowers as they're supposed to be inhabited by spirits.'

'I've heard quite a different version concerning the flower of the baobab tree,' Olivia said thoughtfully, grimacing slightly as the afternoon heat seemed to envelop her, making her body feel clammy beneath her usually cool silk dress. 'They say that if you pick one of its flowers and cast it into a hollow stem, you can make a wish.'

'A wish?' Frances demanded, all ears despite her father's sceptical glance. 'And will your wish come true?'

'I don't know,' Olivia laughed self-consciously. 'I'm only mentioning what I've been told, but I haven't thought it worth repeating until now. It's most probably, just as many legends are, a fabrication.'

'There's a hollow in this stem, so let's make a wish,'

Frances announced with an eagerness that would not be denied as she literally threw herself at her father. 'Help me pick a flower, Daddy, so I can make a wish.'

'You surely don't believe all that nonsense, do you?' he laughed, and his laughter sounded strangely pleasing.

'Sometimes wishes do come true, Daddy,' Frances insisted, and Bernard King's expression sobered as he lifted her on to his shoulder in order to reach one of the flowers. Moments later they watched in solemn silence as she ran across to the hollow in the stem, then, closing her eyes tightly as she wished, she dropped the flower into it. 'Now it's your turn, Olivia.'

'My turn?' she asked, her heart lurching uncomfortably at the thought of provoking further laughter from the man standing beside her.

'Yes,' Frances nodded with childlike innocence. 'Pick a flower and make a wish. Quickly, Olivia!'

Olivia glanced speculatively at the flowers on the overhanging branch, realising, to her embarrassment, that she would never be able to reach one without something to step on.

'Perhaps I could be of some assistance,' Bernard King spoke behind her as he summed up the situation and, before she could protest, his large hands circled her narrow waist and she was lifted effortlessly to within reach of a flower.

Flustered and embarrassed, she fumbled as she picked the delicate blossom and, keeping her face averted, she thanked him and stepped across to the hollow in the stem of the tree. She made a hasty wish, but despite the fact that there was some distance between them, she could still feel the touch of those strong hands about her waist, and the uneven beat of her frightened heart persisted for some time.

'What did you wish for, Miss Logan?' he asked once the act had been accomplished, capturing her wary glance relentlessly with his.

'I wished——'

'Don't tell him, Olivia,' Frances interrupted anxiously, her dark eyes widening. 'If you tell someone what you wished for, then it won't come true.'

'I'd forgotten,' Olivia admitted, her composure in the process of being shattered. Would this day ever end? she wondered as she felt the perspiration trickle down her back. Could this detestable man not find something else to interest him instead of observing her so closely with those frighteningly disturbing dark eyes of his?

'Daddy, it's your turn to make a wish,' Frances insisted, tugging at his hand and mercifully drawing his attention away from Olivia, who was beginning to feel frantic with the desire for escape.

'I think two wishes are enough for one day,' Olivia heard him say. 'Let's take a look at what Evalina has packed into that basket for us.'

A large piece of canvas was spread out on the uneven ground, and being able to help with this was balm to Olivia's nerves. Having a primitive picnic under the baobab tree was nothing new to Bernard King and his daughter, Olivia realised as she joined them on the canvas to explore the contents of the basket.

'Good heavens!' she exclaimed, forgetting her nervousness for a time as she viewed the variety of home-made biscuits, jam tarts and apple pie with disbelief. 'It seems as though we're about to have a party.'

'Evalina's speciality is the apple pie,' Bernard informed her. 'Try some.'

'I will, thank you,' Olivia smiled, helping herself to a slice and biting into it. 'Hm ... it *is* delicious,' she agreed to her hosts's satisfaction.

Not having eaten much at lunch, Olivia discovered that she was hungry. Frances and her father, too, helped themselves to the spread before them as if they had not eaten since breakfast that morning, so Olivia felt quite safe in helping herself to another, and yet another piece of apple pie, which she washed down with the glass of orange juice Bernard King had poured for her.

Frances finally threw herself down on to her stomach beside Olivia, and cupped her chin in her hands as she gazed dreamily out across the veld. Olivia followed the direction of her glance and, to her surprise, saw the sunlight reflected on the water of a dam which was just barely visible through the trees. So this was where Frances and her father swam on those days they came out to the tree on horseback, she thought, closing her eyes against the glare, and becoming aware of a lazy inertia stealing through her limbs.

Some sixth sense warned her that she was being observed and, opening her eyes, she found herself looking directly into Bernard King's infinitely disturbing brown eyes. Perhaps it was the oppressive heat, she told herself after a moment, which had slowed down her reflexes, but she found herself unable to look away for several time-suspending seconds while she experienced the peculiar sensation that she was drowning, and in need of air.

'Would you care for something more to drink?' His deep voice shook through her, bringing her sharply to her senses.

'No, thank you,' she shook her head, drawing the hot air deep into her lungs as she looked away.

'I think it's time we returned home.'

'Must we, Daddy?' Frances demanded frowningly as she sat up, her glance lingering on the shimmering water through the trees.

'We didn't bring swimming gear with us, so we can't go for a swim in the dam,' he said, guessing accurately at the reason for Frances' reluctance to return home. 'I also think that the heat is beginning to affect Miss Logan.'

'It—it is a bit hot,' Olivia admitted, meeting Frances' concerned glance and smiling apologetically.

'It will take quite a while for you to acclimatise,' Bernard

King told her, rising to his feet and extending a large hand towards her. 'Come on.'

He helped her to her feet, his hand gripping hers a moment longer than was necessary before he released it, but Olivia pretended to be unaware of this as she helped him fold up the sheet of canvas while Frances returned the basket to the Land Rover.

The drive back to the homestead seemed to take much less time than the drive out to the tree earlier that afternoon, but then Bernard King had driven at a considerably slower speed as if he had wanted to give her the opportunity to admire the veld in its still practically raw state.

Olivia heard Frances take a swift but soft indrawn breath at the sight of the bottle-green Triumph parked in front of the house. The gauze door leading on to the verandah opened as the Land Rover crunched to a halt beneath the tree where it had been parked earlier that day, and red hair flashed vividly in the sunlight as a slender figure came down the steps and hurried towards them.

'Bernard, where have you been?' that silky voice demanded almost petulantly as they climbed out of the Land Rover.

'Frances and I took Miss Logan to see the old baobab tree,' Bernard informed Ilona Haskins, smiling down at her with a degree of tolerance Olivia had not expected of him.

'Miss Logan?' Ilona queried, her green glance going for the first time to Olivia who walked rather stiffly round to the front of the Land Rover with Frances by her side. 'Oh ...' Ilona's eyes flashed with a hint of venom. 'I didn't notice you. Have you developed a sudden interest in baobab trees, Miss Logan?'

'It is a most unusual tree,' Olivia said lamely, realising only too well that Ilona was hinting at some other reason for her interest in the baobab tree.

'We also made a wish,' Frances chipped in airily, going

into detail about how they had wished on the flower of the baobab.

'Really, Miss Logan,' Ilona arched her perfectly shaped eyebrows derisively, 'aren't you a bit old for such childish games? I can understand Frances indulging in such fantasies, but the thought of a supposedly adult person making a wish on the flower of the baobab is quite laughable!'

Olivia's anger flared, but Frances was quicker off the mark with, 'There's nothing funny about making a wish, and if my wish comes true you won't be standing there laughing!'

'Frances!' Bernard King rapped out disapprovingly. 'Apologise to Miss Haskins at once!'

'I *won't* apologise,' Frances insisted fiercely, stamping her foot to emphasise the fact.

A chilling little silence prevailed before Ilona said with cold disdain, 'Leave her, Bernard. I can guess whom you have to thank for the child's impertinence.'

'Olivia has nothing to do with my not wanting to apologise, so don't you dare blame her!' Frances leapt to Olivia's defence, her face contorted with anger.

'Frances,' Olivia whispered reprovingly, flattered that the child should have defended her, yet afraid of the consequences such behaviour might evoke. But, to her surprise, Bernard threw back his dark head and laughed loudly, displaying strong white teeth and the tanned column of his strong throat.

'Calm down, will you,' he said at last when he had managed to control himself, surprising Olivia even further by adding, 'If I'd believed in the magic of the baobab, I might have made a wish as well. Now, let's go inside and have something cool to drink.'

'I'm afraid I must go now, but it's been a delightful afternoon,' Olivia said quickly, anxious now to escape from Ilona's poisonous glances, and the tension that still hovered like static electricity in the air.

'You can't go yet, Olivia,' Frances pleaded instantly, clutching at Olivia's hand.

'I must, Frances, but I look forward to next Saturday.'

'Next Saturday?' Ilona's eyebrows rose sharply above enquiring green eyes which were directed at the man beside her.

'Frances will be spending her Saturday mornings with Miss Logan in future,' Bernard King explained carelessly.

'Oh ...' said Ilona, clearly taken aback by this disclosure.

'You must come again, Olivia,' Frances insisted, tugging at her hand to draw her attention. 'Next time Daddy could take you for a flip in his aeroplane.'

'I don't think that would be such a good idea,' Olivia laughed self-consciously, aware of Bernard King's silent regard, and the angry sparks emitting from Ilona's eyes. 'I'm terrified just thinking about it.'

'You'd be safe with Daddy,' Frances told her confidently.

'I'm sure I would be,' Olivia smiled shakily, 'but I prefer keeping my feet on the ground, thank you.'

Frances' disappointment was obvious, but she offered no further protest as Olivia murmured a hasty farewell and climbed into her Apache.

Olivia drove back to Louisville with mixed feelings, for despite the fact that she had been so adamant about going to Mountain View only for Frances' sake, she had enjoyed the afternoon to a certain extent and, despite Bernard King's assertion that he tolerated her presence only for the sake of his child, he had been courteous ... and very disturbing. Ilona Haskins' presence at the homestead on their arrival had caused the sparks to fly between Frances and herself, and Olivia dreaded to think what might have happened if Bernard had not saved the situation by laughing it off.

Bernard! Olivia flushed at her audacity to think of him merely as Bernard, but he was the most perplexing man she had ever met, and the most unpredictable. She could still hear his laughter ringing in her ears; deep and throaty, and the memory of it sent a strange quiver along her nerves, making her hands tighten involuntarily on the wheel while her soft mouth hardened.

She was feeling hot and sticky as she parked her car in the garage and locked the doors before rummaging in her handbag for the key to her flat, taking no notice of the flashy red sports car that pulled up beside her at the kerb, and wanting only to escape up to her cool flat.

'Hello there!' Gerald's voice drew her attention. 'It seems I timed it perfectly this time.'

'This time?' she asked, a quick smile flashing across her face.

'I called earlier this afternoon, but found no one at home,' Gerald explained as he climbed out of the car without bothering to open the door.

'I was out at Mountain View.'

'Bernard King's place?' Gerald asked incredulously as he followed her up the steps to her door.

Olivia nodded and explained briefly the incidents which had led up to that afternoon's picnic beneath the baobab tree.

Gerald pinched her arm lightly. 'I told you he was a likeable chap.'

'I didn't find him all that likeable,' Olivia replied coldly. 'Ilona Haskins was there when we arrived back at the house, and she was positively venomous.'

'She would be,' he said, following her inside once she had unlocked the door, and lowering himself into the nearest chair. 'She more or less considers the man her private property.'

'Well, she needn't have any fears where I'm concerned,' Olivia replied adamantly, dropping her bag on to the small table and collapsing wearily into the chair opposite Gerald's. 'I'm very fond of Frances but, as far as Bernard

King is concerned, I couldn't care less whether I never see him again.'

'It does my heart good to hear you say that, so what about having dinner with me this evening?'

'Gerald, I'm rather tired, and . . .' The look of disappointment on his lean, handsome face curved her lips into a smile of resignation. 'If you like, you could stay and have pot luck with me.'

His green eyes sparkled with delight. 'That sounds fine to me.'

In a way it was good to have Gerald with her for a few hours. His company was relaxing and the tension which had plagued her so incessantly during that afternoon uncoiled within her until she found herself laughing almost hilariously at silly little remarks he made; remarks which would not normally have drawn more than a chuckle from her. She was tired, she realised eventually, and the heat in the veld had sapped her strength, leaving her close to exhaustion.

Gerald did not stay late and whether, because of her tiredness, he had interpreted her behaviour to mean something more, she could not say, but he tried to draw her into his arms as they stood in the shadowy doorway.

'Don't spoil our friendship,' she pleaded instantly, pulling away from him before his lips could touch hers.

'You're not very good for my ego, you know,' he mocked gently, not relinquishing his grip on her arms.

'I'm sorry, but I think it best that you know exactly where you stand.'

'And where *do* I stand?'

Olivia raised her tired glance to his, the light from the lounge casting shadows beneath her eyes and making them appear larger than they actually were. 'There can never be anything more than friendship between us, and I don't care for meaningless flirtations.'

Gerald's expression sobered considerably. 'I wasn't flirting with you, Olivia.'

'You're not serious either,' she contradicted, a touch of humour curving her lips despite the fact that she wished he would go and leave her to shower and crawl into bed.

'You're a cool little creature, my dear, and I can see it will take someone far more determined than I am to win your love,' he said gravely, releasing her arms. 'In the meantime, you won't mind if I hang around, will you?'

'I won't mind at all, just as long as you don't expect more of me than I can give,' she laughed lightly, pushing him playfully out the door. 'Goodnight, Gerald.'

To her relief he went without any protest, waving as he reached the bottom of the steps, and leaping into his hoodless car like an energetic boy before he started the engine and roared off down the silent street. Olivia sighed and shook her head. He was an absolute dear, but he could never mean more to her than just a friend. It was a pity, but there it was.

CHAPTER FIVE

VIVIEN telephoned Olivia at the shop the Monday morning and, as Olivia had suspected, her trip out to the farm became the first topic of conversation, and she was instantly on her guard as Vivien said:

'I heard all about Bernard taking you out to the old baobab tree on Saturday, and Frances also told me how the two of you made a wish.'

'I found it very interesting to learn of the various legends attached to the baobab,' Olivia replied politely, hoping that that was all Frances had divulged.

'I bet Bernard never mentioned the legend in which he became involved as a young man.'

'Which one was that?' Olivia asked, not particularly interested in Bernard King, but curious about the legend.

'Well, it's said that, if a man drinks an extract made of the bark of the boabab, he'll become mighty and strong,' said Vivien, laughing softly. 'During one of the rituals of the Venda people, Bernard was given this potion to drink and, because of his enormous physique, we've teased him about it ever since.'

'No, he never told me,' Olivia said, suppressing a giggle at the thought of sceptical Bernard King indulging in one of the fanciful legends of the Venda tribe.

'By the way,' Vivien interrupted her thoughts, 'my tapestry is completed. How far have you got with yours?'

Olivia glanced at her own tapestry on the counter beside her. 'I'm finishing it off at the moment.'

'Good! We can send them off together then to have them framed.' There was a slight pause before Vivien continued,

'Look, I actually telephoned to ask if you were free on Wednesday evening. Are you, Olivia?'

'Yes, I am ... why?' she asked hesitantly.

'I would like you to come and have dinner with Peter and me,' came Vivien's surprising reply. 'It will be quite informal, and I've talked so much about you that Peter is dying to meet you. Will you come?'

Olivia's mind raced uncomfortably, but she consoled herself with the thought that Vivien had not mentioned her brother at all, and, assuming that he would not be present, she said: 'I would like to very much, thank you.'

'Do you know where we live?' Vivien wanted to know, the excited tremor in her voice coming clearly across the line.

'I'm afraid I don't.'

'Well, if you turn left at the old stone church in the main street, and then——' She broke off abruptly and continued hastily with, 'Never mind, I'll come and fetch you at ... six-thirty?'

'That sounds fine, but I'm sure if you gave me directions I should find——'

'No, no, I'll come and fetch you,' Vivien insisted. 'I wouldn't want you to get lost, and Peter could always take you back if he isn't called out during dinner. See you on Wednesday, then.'

She rang off abruptly, almost as if she was afraid that Olivia would change her mind, but Olivia merely smiled as she replaced the receiver, and found herself looking forward to spending an evening in the company of Vivien and her husband.

Tante Maria came into the shop that afternoon and lowered her plump figure in the pink overall on to the stool beside the counter as she handed a letter to Olivia.

'It somehow managed to get in among our post,' she explained, eyeing the envelope with as much curiosity as Olivia. 'Aren't you going to open it and see what it's about?'

Unable to suppress a smile, Olivia tore open the envelope and extracted a single sheet of paper. As she read through it swiftly, the frown on her brow cleared slightly.

'It's from the property agent in Johannesburg,' she explained to the curious Tante Maria. 'They've found a buyer for my aunt's house and they want me to go through to Johannesburg as soon as possible to sign the papers for the sale to go through.'

'When will you go?' Tante Maria wanted to know, shifting herself into a more comfortable position on the stool.

'I don't fancy travelling there and back in one day,' Olivia replied slowly, returning the letter to the envelope. 'Perhaps if I left just after lunch on Sunday, then I could stay over at a hotel, see the agent on Monday morning, and come back that afternoon.'

'That would be the wisest thing to do,' the older woman agreed, frowning suddenly. 'What about your shop?'

'I'll just have to close it for the day,' Olivia sighed, unable to think of anyone whom she could ask to help out for the day.

'You could always leave your keys with me so that, if anyone wanted something urgently, I could slip away quickly and help them.'

'That's very kind of you, Tante Maria,' Olivia thanked her, 'but I think Louisville can do without its bookshop for one day without falling apart!'

Tante Maria agreed wholeheartedly and remained a few minutes longer to ask how Olivia's week-end had been before she heaved herself on to her feet and made her way reluctantly back to their shop next door. Olivia watched her go, considering herself lucky to have two such nice people close by to whom she could turn for advice if she should ever need it, but her train of thought was interrupted as a burly farmer entered the shop to collect his magazines.

Wednesday evening arrived almost too quickly for Olivia as she stood in front of her wardrobe and contemplated which dress to wear. Vivien had stipulated that it would be informal, but Olivia glanced ruefully at her clothes, realising that she had day dresses and evening dresses, but nothing in between for an informal evening at someone's home. If only she had had time to do some shopping, she thought agitatedly, determined now to do a tour of the shops while in Johannesburg that coming Monday.

Deciding eventually on her plain blue chiffon which was not as elaborate as her other evening dresses, she slipped it over her head and pulled up the zip before examining herself critically in the mirror. The colour matched her eyes, the sales lady had said when Olivia had bought it, and she had to admit that the style, plain though it was, did something for her almost boyish figure.

Glancing at the alarm clock beside her bed, she hastily checked her make-up, pulled a comb through her hair which had grown over the past weeks to fall softly into her neck, and fastened a silver bracelet on to her wrist. She just had time to grab her stole and purse before she glimpsed Vivien's small blue Fiat coming down the street and, taking another swift glance at herself in the mirror, she hurried down to where Vivien was busy parking her car.

'Hm ... you look nice,' Vivien smiled, coming forward to meet her, 'but you're so small and slender that I feel like an elephant beside you.'

'Nonsense, Vivien,' Olivia protested as they climbed into the Fiat. 'You have a lovely figure, and I'd give anything to be a little taller.'

Vivien started the car and sent a humorous glance in Olivia's direction. 'So you could have reached the baobab tree flower without assistance?'

'Oh ...' Olivia felt her cheeks redden and looked away as she recalled how Bernard King had had to lift her in order to pick a flower. 'I should have known you would have been told about that. Did Mr King...?'

'Frances told me,' Vivien replied quickly, taking in the look of relief on Olivia's face before returning her attention to the road ahead. 'That child is extraordinarily fond of you, you know.'

'I know, and it frightens me a little,' Olivia admitted, her colour returning to normal.

'Good heavens, why?'

'I don't know,' Olivia shrugged. 'Perhaps I'm afraid of hurting her some day.'

'If Bernard had married again then Frances might have turned out quite differently, but he's thirty-eight now, and I'm beginning to think that he prefers living the way he does,' Vivien sighed, her lips tightening. 'Of course, if Ilona had her way she would have been mistress of Mountain View years ago and, quite frankly, I dread the day when that happens.'

'Do you think it might?' Olivia asked conversationally, not caring one way or the other whether Bernard King married Ilona Haskins or not. Frances would, of course, be the one to suffer, but that was not really her concern, was it?

'Bernard doesn't say much,' she heard Vivien remark disconsolately, 'but Ilona drops enough hints that their relationship is developing in that direction.'

They arrived at Vivien's house within a short space of time, and Olivia paid little attention to the large white Mercedes parked at the gate as she feasted her eyes on Vivien's rose garden, and the modern, two-storied house with its large windows and glass doors leading out on to a terraced garden which was bathed in gold at that moment by the last rays of the sun.

'This way,' said Vivien, guiding Olivia towards the entrance of the house with its panelled glass windows on either side of the door, but, in the spacious entrance hall, the sound of a familiar deep voice made her halt abruptly and, but for Vivien's detaining hand on her arm, she would have turned and fled instead of allowing herself to be led into the large, airy living-room where Bernard King sat talking to a lean, fair-haired man. At the sound of their footsteps on the tiled floor, both men glanced up and rose to their feet, and Olivia felt her knees shaking beneath her weight as Vivien said: 'Peter, this is Olivia Logan. Olivia, my husband.'

'Well, at last I have the pleasure of meeting you, Olivia,' Peter O'Brien smiled warmly, clasping her hand in his and staring at her with interest deepening in his blue eyes. 'I've heard so much about you from both Vivien and Frances that I feel as though we're old friends.'

Conscious of Bernard King's glowering expression, she smiled up at the man before her with a little more warmth than usual. 'It's kind of you to say so, Dr O'Brien.'

'Peter ... please,' he corrected swiftly, releasing her hand. 'No one calls me Dr O'Brien except my patients, and you're far too healthy-looking to ever be that.' He gestured towards the man beside him. 'You have met Bernard, I believe?'

'Yes,' she murmured, meeting the fierce intensity of those dark eyes with a calmness that was deceiving. 'Good evening, Mr King.'

His eyes were instantly mocking. 'Good evening, Miss Logan.'

'For goodness' sake!' Vivien exploded beside Olivia. 'Drop this "Mr King" and "Miss Logan" nonsense, both of you, or I shall choke on the dinner I've taken so much time to prepare!'

The tension eased slightly as Olivia was shown to a chair, but Bernard remained standing, his empty glass in his hand. 'I'm about to help myself to another glass of wine. Could I get the same for you ... Olivia?'

The sound of her name on his lips jarred her nerves, but she managed to smile stiffly. 'That would be nice, thank you.'

'I could do with a refill myself, so I'll get Vivien's,' said

Peter, rising to his feet and following Bernard from the room.

'You never told me that—that your brother would be here as well,' Olivia accused the moment they were alone.

Vivien leaned back in her chair and crossed her shapely legs. 'Would you have come had I told you?'

'No,' Olivia replied with complete honesty.

'There you are, then,' Vivien smiled with satisfaction. 'He's not such an ogre, Olivia. You'll see, my dear.'

Olivia remained unconvinced, but the men returned and they were forced to discontinue their conversation. To her dismay, Bernard did not return to the chair he had occupied before their arrival, but, after handing her her glass of wine, he lowered himself into the chair directly beside her own, making her painfully aware of his large, imposing frame in grey slacks and matching jacket with the whiteness of his open-necked shirt accentuating the darkness of his bearded features.

'What do you think of Louisville, Olivia, after living in Johannesburg for most of your life?' Peter brought the conversation round to her eventually.

'I think it's a lovely town,' she replied truthfully, conscious of Bernard's dark, enquiring gaze resting on her as she continued. 'It's very quiet, but I like it that way.'

'Does the lack of night-life not trouble you?' that deep voice shivered along her sensitive nerves, forcing her to glance in his direction.

'I never had much experience of Johannesburg's night-life, so I don't miss it at all.'

'I bet you left a few broken hearts behind,' Peter observed mischievously.

'Peter, you're embarrassing Olivia,' Vivien interrupted, noticing the pinkness of Olivia's cheeks.

'Nonsense,' Peter insisted jovially as he leaned forward in his chair and pursued the subject. 'Did you leave a few broken hearts behind?'

'None that I can think of,' Olivia answered, wishing that she was not so conscious of Bernard's unfaltering gaze.

'Oh, come now,' Peter laughed, his eyes crinkling at the corners. 'A girl as pretty as you must have had a retinue of admirers.'

Olivia's lips curved into an involuntary smile. 'You flatter me, but I'm afraid I—I never had much time to indulge in that kind of occupation.'

'What could have kept you so fully occupied, I wonder?' Bernard remarked beside her with a hint of sarcasm in his voice.

'Really, Bernard, that's none of your business,' Vivien sprang to her defence instantly, her brows drawn into a straight line of disapproval that made the likeness between her and her brother so very obvious.

'I was merely curious,' Bernard replied, quite unperturbed. 'But if Olivia prefers to be mysterious about her past, then it's up to her to say so.'

'There's nothing mysterious about my past,' Olivia protested, her fingers tightening on the stem of her glass. 'I had my job as a librarian, and my books at home.'

'Your parents?' Bernard persisted, his glance compelling.

'They died when I was two, and I was brought up by my mother's sister,' the words came out jerkily.

His eyes darkened perceptibly. 'I'm sorry.'

'And so you should be,' Vivien interrupted forcefully.

'It doesn't matter,' Olivia said quickly, anxious now to ease the tension between Bernard King and herself as he rapped out yet another query.

'Your aunt? Is she still living in Johannesburg?'

'She died about ten months ago,' Olivia confessed, lowering her lashes swiftly to hide the pain from Bernard's prying eyes.

Brother and sister glared at each other as Peter stepped hastily into the breach. 'You must think us brutes to question you like this on a subject that must still be painful to you, Olivia.'

'I'm glad it was you who said that, Peter, because that's what I've been trying to point out for the past half hour,' Vivien said icily before Olivia had time to scrape together a reply. 'Don't think too badly of them, Olivia. They're not always so callous.'

It felt to Olivia as if the pleasant, restful evening she had envisaged had suddenly exploded into a million fragments, leaving her tense and withdrawn from the other occupants in this beautiful living-room with its cream-coloured furnishings and wine-red curtains at the windows. To her relief the conversation at the dinner-table remained light and amusing, and although Bernard King was the only one who appeared to notice that she had shrunk into a world of her own, he fortunately did not bring it to the notice of Peter and Vivien, but Olivia, seated opposite him, was constantly aware of his dark eyes regarding her so intently from time to time, and aware, too, of an uneasiness she could not explain.

'Have you completed your tapestry?' Vivien asked Olivia suddenly when they reached the coffee stage, and Olivia squirmed inwardly when everyone's attention was all at once focussed on her.

'Yes, I have,' she replied, swallowing nervously.

'Good,' Vivien said brightly. 'I'll collect yours tomorrow and send it off with mine.'

'Well, I ...' The words seemed to dry up in her throat and she had to force herself to continue. 'I have to be in Johannesburg on Monday, so I thought perhaps I could take them myself.'

Vivien's dark glance sharpened. 'Were you going to travel by car?'

Olivia nodded. 'I thought I'd leave Sunday afternoon and stay over in a hotel so there wouldn't be so much travelling all in one day.'

'But why go all that way by car when you could fly there on Monday morning with Bernard?' Vivien argued, and Olivia's heart almost leapt out of her throat as she saw

Vivien glance across at her brother. 'You are still going through to Johannesburg on Monday, aren't you?'

Bernard nodded slowly. 'I am, and you're welcome to come with me, Olivia.'

'Oh, but I couldn't! I mean——' She broke off abruptly, realising how ungrateful she must sound judging by the hint of mockery in Bernard's eyes. 'I should hate to be an imposition,' she ended off lamely.

'Nonsense!' Vivien protested, dismissing Olivia's argument with an imperious wave of her hand. 'It would be silly for you to drive all that way when you could get there so much quicker in Bernard's Cessna.'

'Olivia doesn't care for flying,' Bernard said smoothly, and Olivia was almost certain that this frightful man opposite her was laughing at her again behind his beard.

'It's not that,' Olivia said at last, her cheeks scarlet. 'I just don't like inconveniencing anyone.'

'Then you will go with Bernard?' Vivien demanded.

Olivia sighed inwardly and nodded. 'Thank you.'

'Wonderful!' Vivien exclaimed, leaning her elbows on the table. 'Now, what about your shop on Monday?'

'I thought I'd just close it for the day.'

'No, you won't,' Vivien shook her head firmly. 'I'll come in on Saturday morning so you can show me all there is to know, then I could help out on Monday while you're away.'

Olivia drew her breath in sharply. 'I'd never dream of of allowing you to do any such thing!'

'But I insist!'

Peter, who had been listening silently to their conversation, shook his fair head at last and laughed shortly. 'When Vivien says, "But I insist" in that tone of voice, you don't stand a chance, Olivia, so give in gracefully and let her have her way.'

Olivia leaned back weakly in her chair and smiled across at him with a little gesture of defeat. 'It seems I shall have to.'

When they returned to the living-room a few minutes later, Olivia wondered confusedly why she had allowed herself to be forced into taking this trip to Johannesburg with Bernard King. It was bad enough that she had to tolerate his presence there that evening, but to spend several hours alone with him in an aeroplane would be absolutely unbearable, she decided, shrinking mentally from the mere thought of it.

The clock on the mantelshelf finally chimed ten and, sighing inwardly with relief, Olivia rose to her feet. 'Vivien, it's been a lovely evening,' she said politely, 'but I must go home now.'

Her statement brought everyone to their feet but, instead of Peter, it was Bernard who said: 'I must go as well, so I'll give you a lift home, Olivia.'

'Oh, no!' she cried in alarm, then, meeting his challenging glance, her chin rose with a measure of defiance. 'I mean . . . thank you.'

Collecting her wrap and her bag, Olivia allowed Bernard to guide her out to the Mercedes parked at the gate, and she wondered now why she had not guessed earlier that evening that it would belong to him.

'Goodnight, Olivia,' said Vivien, glancing in at the window as Bernard climbed in at the other side and inserted the key in the ignition. 'I hope we're going to see more of you now that you know where we live.'

'That's very kind of you, Vivien,' Olivia smiled, glancing beyond her at the tall, fair man who stood grinning down at them both. 'Goodnight, Peter.'

'Goodnight, my dear,' he said warmly, placing an arm about Vivien's waist, 'and don't let Vivien bully you too much.'

'If you're not careful, you'll have a black eye tomorrow,' Vivien threatened with mock severity.

'See what I mean?' Peter wanted to know, dodging a badly aimed blow.

'I think we'd better go before these two really come to blows,' Bernard remarked in a voice loud enough for the others to hear before he started the car amidst the sound of laughter, and shouts of 'Goodnight'.

Olivia waved for the last time, but as the car gathered speed along the darkened street, the silence between Bernard and herself kept her rigid and tense in her seat.

'You're very quiet, Olivia?' he said at last. 'Do you find us a little overpowering?'

She found them all downright domineering, but she heard herself stammer foolishly, 'Not—not really.'

'Then what were you thinking about?'

'I—I was merely thinking that I'm taking you out of your way,' she said the first thing that came into her head.

'Were you?' he asked, his voice tinged with humour in the darkness of the car. 'Have you lost your sense of direction?'

'I ... beg your pardon?'

'I have to pass your shop on my way out of town,' he explained dryly.

'Oh ... yes, of course,' she laughed, kicking herself mentally. 'How silly of me.'

'Has Vivien talked you into entering your tapestry for the Show?' he asked, changing the subject.

'Definitely not!'

The light from the dashboard illuminated his face as he glanced at her briefly. 'I thought she might have, seeing that you're having yours framed with hers.'

'It's my first attempt at tapestry making, and I really only made it for my own amusement.'

'There's no harm in entering it,' Bernard persisted.

'Oh, please ... I couldn't!' she argued, relieved at the sight of the single lamp above the door of her shop which lit up the pavement.

The coldness of the door-handle was against her fingers even before he had stopped the car but, anticipating her action, he caught hold of her wrist and forced her to remain seated.

'You know,' he said harshly, releasing her as he switched off the engine and turned to face her, 'I don't think I've ever met anyone as reserved as you are. Most women can't wait to display their handiwork, and then proceed to bore you to tears about the minutest details.'

Olivia shrank back from the bearded face so close to hers, realising that he was intent upon reading her expression, but knowing that he was incapable of doing so while she had the advantage of the light behind her.

Gaining confidence from this fact, she said: 'It does make a difference, I suppose, if one is talented in one way or another, but I can't claim to be particularly talented in any of the arts or crafts.'

'Perhaps you're talented in other fields.'

'I can't say I've discovered any latent talents.'

'You're good with children.'

'I haven't much experience——'

'There you go again,' he accused harshly.

'There I go again *what*?' she asked with a hint of anger, intensely aware of his arm resting along the back of the seat behind her shoulders.

'Talking yourself into insignificance,' he explained roughly. 'I think you haven't given yourself the opportunity to discover just what you are capable of.'

'That's not true!'

'I think it is.' The arm behind her moved slightly and she stiffened as his hand touched her shoulder. 'You've done wonders for Frances in a very short time.'

'Frances is different,' she argued in a choked voice.

'How different?'

'I—I don't know,' she shrugged lightly, every nerve in her body reacting violently to his touch. 'I can't explain.'

'Try.'

Olivia glanced down at her hands in the darkness as she

felt them trembling in her lap. 'I think perhaps she reminds me a little of myself.'

'In what way?'

If only he would remove that large, disturbing hand from her shoulder, she prayed as she said breathlessly, 'Oh, I don't know. Does it matter?'

'You tell me,' he said harshly after a momentary pause, and then, suddenly, she was free and he was walking round the front of the car to open the door for her.

'Thank you for the lift,' she said nervously as she stood beside him on the pavement.

'I'm coming to your door with you.'

'That's really not necessary,' she protested weakly, wishing he would just go away and leave her alone.

'Must you always argue?' he demanded forcefully, taking her arm and marching her up the steps to her flat where he removed the key from her trembling hands and proceeded to unlock the door. Switching on the light, he looked a long way down at her and asked, 'Do you think you could be out at my place before six on Monday morning?'

'Yes, I think I could manage that.'

'It's a little more than a two-hour flight to Johannesburg, so we have to make an early start,' he explained.

'Yes, of course.'

There was a frightening little pause before he said: 'Goodnight, Olivia.'

'Goodnight, Mr King.'

'Bernard,' he corrected mockingly, and a wave of desperation swamped Olivia as she stared up at him and found nothing to attract her in that bearded face.

'Anything,' she thought helplessly. 'I'll do anything just to get rid of him.'

'Bernard,' she echoed, using his name for the first time, and feeling her cheeks grow hot under his forceful gaze, but an eternity seemed to pass before he nodded briefly and left.

Olivia had closed the door behind her and was leaning weakly against it even before he had started his car and driven away. She had managed somehow to get through this evening, but how was she going to endure four hours of his solitary company that coming Monday? She could change her plans and plead that she was feeling ill, she supposed, but, knowing Vivien, she would have Peter there within a flash, and it would not take him long to discover that she suffered from nothing more serious than 'cold feet'.

'Oh, damn!' she muttered, pressing her fingertips against her temples. Why couldn't they just leave her alone instead of organising her into situations she had no wish to become involved in?

Vivien arrived at the shop at eight-thirty sharp that Saturday morning, and Bernard arrived with Frances a half hour later. Apart from enquiring whether their arrangement was still in order for that coming Monday, he said little else and left soon afterwards.

'I wish Bernard would shave that horrible beard off,' Vivien muttered the moment he had gone. 'I wouldn't be able to stand it if Peter were to grow one.'

'Daddy's beard tickles,' Frances giggled. 'Do you like a man with a beard, Olivia?'

'I don't particularly care for a beard,' Olivia replied carefully, not wishing to become involved in a discussion concerning Bernard King's appearance, but her heart lurched uncomfortably when she noted the flash of humour in Vivien's eyes.

There was fortunately no opportunity to continue the discussion, for they were kept busy during the next few hours, and the expressions on the faces of some of Olivia's customers were quite comical when they found Vivien as well as Frances in the shop that morning. Vivien was quite unperturbed, however, and Olivia found that she grasped everything without much difficulty, looking very much as if she was enjoying herself in her new role as assistant shop-keeper.

To Olivia's surprise, Ilona Haskins walked into the shop just after ten that morning, and Olivia marvelled at this woman's ability to always appear so cool and unaffected by the sometimes suffocating heat.

'So this is your bookshop, is it?' Ilona remarked after a perfunctory greeting, glancing about her loftily. 'It's not very big, is it?'

'It's quite big enough for me to cope with, Miss Haskins,' Olivia replied coolly. 'Was there anything you wanted?'

'Oh, goodness, no!' Ilona laughed derisively. 'I seldom read, and the magazines I require are mailed to me directly.' Ignoring Olivia, she looked directly at Frances who had stood silently beside Olivia from the moment Ilona had entered the shop. Ilona's perfectly shaped lips parted in a smile that never reached her cold green eyes. 'I saw your father in town and, as I'm going out to the farm a little later, I told him I would pick you up and take you home.'

Olivia felt Frances stiffen beside her, but at that moment Vivien emerged from the back where she had been making tea. 'You're not, you know,' Vivien replied to Ilona's state-ment in a cool voice. '*I'm* taking Frances home when the shop closes.'

'Oh!' Ilona was momentarily startled by Vivien's pres-ence, but her eyes hardened perceptibly despite the artificial smile that curved her lips. 'Hello, Vivien. What are you doing here?'

'I'm helping out so that I can take over on Monday when Olivia flies to Johannesburg with Bernard,' Vivien replied calmly as she placed the tray of tea on the counter.

'Is Bernard flying to Johannesburg on Monday?' Ilona wanted to know, clearly taken aback.

'Yes,' Vivien nodded with a satisfied smile. 'Didn't you know?'

'No, I didn't,' Ilona said stiffly, her cold glance raking

Olivia. 'I was hoping I could go with him on this occasion as I have some urgent business to attend to in Johannesburg.'

Olivia, seeking escape from a situation she dreaded, said hastily, 'Miss Haskins, I don't mind making other——'

'I'm afraid it's out of the question this time, Ilona,' Vivien cut across Olivia's words with that immovable determination Olivia was beginning to know so well.

'So it seems,' Ilona remarked softly, her chilling glance sending a shiver along Olivia's spine. 'Well, I'll say "cheerio", then.'

She swept out of the shop without a backward glance, leaving behind only a subtle hint of her expensive perfume to remind them of her presence. A frightening realisation took shape in Olivia's mind as she watched Vivien pour the tea quite calmly as if nothing out of the ordinary had happened. Ilona Haskins might have considered her a negligible nuisance on the first two occasions they had met, but now she was an enemy trespassing on a territory which Ilona Haskins had marked off as 'Private Property'.

'Aunty Viv,' Frances interrupted the uneasy silence as she wriggled herself on to the stool to reach her tea on the counter, 'I didn't know you were going out to the farm this afternoon.'

'Neither did I, pet,' Vivien replied instantly, her humorous glance meeting Olivia's briefly over the child's head. 'Let's just call it a decision made on the spur of the moment.'

CHAPTER SIX

OLIVIA arrived at Mountain View just before six that Monday morning while the dew still covered the earth and lay sparkling in the first, slanted rays of the rising sun. She parked her car beneath the old jacaranda tree and locked it, dropping the keys into her sling bag which she hitched on to her shoulder, and clutching the small, rolled-up parcel containing the tapestries. Birds fluttered noisily in the tree above her and, in the distance the sound of bellowing cattle echoed out across the awakening bushveld. She paused for a moment, drawing the fresh, spicy air into her lungs as she watched a thin spiral of smoke rising upwards into the clear blue sky from one of the homestead chimneys.

How wonderful it must be to live in such peaceful surroundings, to awaken each morning to the sounds of nature beginning to stir after the long night, she thought, reluctant to enter the house and announce herself as she glanced about her with a peculiar longing stirring inside her.

The gauze door on the verandah banged loudly, disturbing her thoughts, but the sound of heavy footsteps crunching on the gravel made her swing round sharply to face the tall stranger approaching her. Her frantic glance took in the dark grey business suit and the polished leather shoes before sweeping upwards again to the rugged yet strangely attractive features. Dark eyes captured her startled gaze in which recognition was beginning to dawn, but the sound of that deep-throated voice was unmistakable.

'Good morning, Olivia.'

'Good morning, Mr King,' she replied, stifling the giggle that rose in her throat as she stared up into his clean-shaven face, seeing for the first time the hard, square line of his jaw, and the firm, perfectly chiselled mouth with the hint of sensuality in the curve of the lower lip.

'I thought it was decided the other night that we would dispense with the "Mr King" nonsense,' he demanded abruptly.

'Yes ... Bernard,' she managed, swallowing down yet another bout of laughter, but she did not succeed in veiling her eyes swiftly enough.

'What are you laughing at?' he demanded sternly, his glance raking her from top to toe in her apricot slacks and matching short-sleeved top.

'You,' she blurted out the truth, no longer able to check the laughter that bubbled past her lips. 'You've shaved your beard off.'

His lips tightened ominously. 'Is that so amusing?'

'I'm sorry,' she choked back a giggle. 'It's just that it—makes you look so—so different.'

'I suppose it does,' he agreed after a moment, fingering his jaw with a large, rough hand before he frowned down at her once more. 'Now, if you don't mind, could we get a move on?'

'Yes, of course,' Olivia muttered, pulling herself together with an effort as he led her towards the Land Rover parked beneath a pergola on which the scarlet bougainvillaea ranked profusely.

They drove in silence past the stables and outhouses towards his private airstrip which Olivia discovered was some distance beyond the house. The red and white Cessna awaited them and, for one frightening moment, Olivia felt her stomach muscles tightening painfully, but Bernard's hand was beneath her elbow and she was being propelled firmly towards the two-seater plane. He helped her into the seat beside him, and brushed aside her fumbling hands to fasten the safety belt securely before he did the same with his own.

'Put this on so we can talk to each other without having

to shout above the noise of the engine,' he instructed, passing her a pair of earphones similar to the one he had already placed on his head, and, while he was still carrying out this task, the engine sprang to life, setting the plane vibrating beneath her, and she looked up to see the propeller whirling about with increasing speed. Bernard made radio contact with his air base and an aeronautical discussion followed which meant little or nothing to Olivia as she took a deep breath to still the pounding of her heart. So engrossed was she in calming herself that she almost jumped violently when he addressed her suddenly. 'Have you ever flown before, Olivia?'

'No, never,' she shook her head, wishing herself anywhere but there with him at that moment.

'You're not afraid, are you?'

It was a challenging question, and one which she could not answer at once as she met his dark, penetrating glance. Lowering her lashes after what seemed an eternity, she glimpsed those strong hands on the controls, and her fluttering nerves seemed to sort themselves into their proper order so that she finally said, with complete honesty, 'No, I'm not afraid.'

Bernard nodded briefly, setting the plane in motion. On the smooth gravel runway, he opened up the throttle and the Cessna leapt forward, gathering speed with every second until he pulled back the stick, lifting the nose of the plane, and leaving the earth behind as they soared upwards. Olivia held her breath, watching the ground fall away beneath them, and closing her eyes momentarily as they skimmed the tall trees at the end of the runway. They gained height gradually, giving her the peculiar sensation that she was floating through the air, and it was not until they had gained the required height that she broke the silence between them.

'Do most of the farmers in this district have their own planes?' she asked, watching Louisville disappear beneath them.

'I think I'm the only one in this area who has a plane, but then I'm keen on flying,' he admitted.

'It must save you a lot of time.'

'It does,' he said, and the next instant Olivia clutched at the sides of her seat, her cheeks paling visibly as the plane rocked and bumped when it was caught in air-pockets over the mountain peaks. Bernard's expression registered unexpected concern as he glanced at her. 'Are you feeling all right?'

'I think I can stand the occasional bump,' she replied, relaxing now as the rocking motion ceased. 'Just don't do any aerobatic tricks, will you.'

'I shan't,' he smiled briefly. 'A green complexion wouldn't suit you at all.'

'And neither would it impress Mr Roberts,' she quipped back lightly, relaxing in her seat once more.

'Roberts?' he questioned, his glance sharpening.

'The estate agent I have to see.'

'Are you buying property?'

'Selling,' she smiled ruefully. 'I had to put my aunt's house up for sale when I moved to Louisville.'

'Has this Mr Roberts found a buyer?' Bernard asked with interest, returning his glance to the numerous dials in front of him.

'It appears so,' she told him, studying his profile unobtrusively and wondering irrationally why he had chosen to hide those attractive features beneath a frightful beard. 'That's why I'm going to see him. My signature is needed to complete the sale.'

Bernard nodded absently and Olivia concentrated on the scenery so far below her. They were leaving the bushveld behind them, and flying instead over irrigated lands, winding rivers and fertile valleys. The Cessna's engine droned on almost monotonously as the sun rose higher in the cloudless sky, sending its warmth into the chilly cabin and relaxing Olivia's tense body.

She listened attentively as Bernard pointed out several

interesting landmarks, and she was surprised to discover that they had been flying for almost an hour when he said: 'If you look below us you'll see Potgietersrus.'

Olivia stared at the picturesque town with its sub-tropical gardens and tree-lined streets. She had driven through it several times during the past months, but there seemed to be nothing familiar about it at that moment.

'It looks different from up here, doesn't it,' she remarked tentatively, expecting to be mocked, but Bernard merely nodded his dark head.

'Did you know that it was originally called Piet Potgietersrus?' he asked with a suggestion of a smile curving his lips.

'No,' she admitted, 'but I know it was named after Commandant-General Piet Potgieter.'

'Clever girl,' he grinned, his eyes crinkling slightly at the outer corners, and she wondered for a moment whether he was mocking her as usual.

'They farm mostly with tobacco and groundnuts in this area, don't they?' she continued to question him as she stared down at the neatly fenced off lands below them.

'That, as well as citrus, cotton and maize.'

They flew in silence for some minutes before she asked the question which had been hovering on her lips for some time.

'Who's taking Frances back to school this morning?'

His eyebrows rose slightly, and Olivia was just beginning to think that he would tell her to mind her own business when he said: 'I took her back yesterday afternoon.'

'I don't suppose she was very pleased about *that*.'

'No,' he admitted, his lips twisting wryly, 'but it's not the first time I've had to take her in on a Sunday afternoon when I've flown to Johannesburg the following day.'

They lapsed into another lengthy silence, but Olivia finally witnessed something from the air which made her gasp involuntarily with delight. Pretoria lay stretched out

TAKE FOUR
BEST SELLER ROMANCES
FREE!

Best Sellers are for the true romantic! These stories are our favourite Romance titles re-published by popular demand.

And to introduce to you this superb series, we'll send you four Best Sellers absolutely FREE when you complete and return this card.

We're so confident that you will enjoy Best Sellers that we'll also reserve a subscription for you to the Mills & Boon Reader Service, which means you could enjoy...

Four new novels sent direct to you every two months (before they're available in the shops).

Free postage and packing we pay all the extras.

Free regular Newsletter packed with special offers, competitions, author news and much, much more.

CLAIM YOUR FREE GIFTS OVERLEAF

Mills & Boon — FREE BOOKS CERTIFICATE

YES! Please send me my four **FREE** Best Sellers together with my **FREE** gifts. Please also reserve me a special Reader Service Subscription. If I decide to subscribe, I shall receive four superb Best Sellers every other month for just £6 postage and packing free. If I decide not to subscribe I shall write to you within 10 days. Any **FREE** books and gifts will remain mine to keep. I understand that I am under no obligation whatsoever - I may cancel or suspend my subscription at any time simply by writing to you. *I am over 18 years of age.*

6AIB

NAME _____ Signature _____

ADDRESS _____

_____ POSTCODE _____

POST TODAY
and we'll send you this cuddly Teddy Bear.

PLUS a free mystery gift!
we all love mysteries, so as well as the FREE books and cuddly Teddy, there's an intriguing mystery gift specially for you.

MILLS & BOON
FREEPOST
P.O. BOX 236
CROYDON
CR9 9EL

NO
STAMP
NEEDED

below them, its streets lined with purple-flowering jacaranda trees which were the trademark of this beautiful city. On Meintjeskop to the left stood the Union Buildings, built in a modified Grecian style with pillared pavilions flanking a colonnaded semi-circular central structure with two domed towers, and below the building the terraced gardens stretched down as far as Church Street. Directly ahead, and slightly to the right, stood the colossal granite-structured Voortrekker Monument with the laager of ox wagons circling it.

'We're almost at our destination,' Bernard remarked moments before requesting permission to land from air control, and a few minutes later they touched down at the Halfway House Grand Central Airport.

Bernard unfastened Olivia's seat-belt and helped her alight before he ushered her across the tarmac towards the dark blue Mercedes he had hired for the day.

'It's just after eight,' he said as he climbed into the car beside her and flicked back the cuff of his jacket to glance at the gold watch fastened to his strong wrist. 'What time do you have to be at Mr Roberts' office?'

'No specific time,' Olivia replied carefully. 'All I told him on the telephone was that I'd see him during the course of the morning.'

'In that case we can stop somewhere and have breakfast,' Bernard announced, starting the car.

Olivia glanced at him in alarm. 'Please, that's not necessary. I——'

'You may not be hungry, but I am,' he interrupted firmly, and she knew by the sudden hardening of his jaw that it would be useless to argue further.

He was almost a complete stranger with his beard shaved off, she thought distractedly, glancing at him surreptitiously as they drove the remaining distance to Johannesburg. She could see now that there was a strong likeness between him and Vivien, except that Vivien's features were more refined, more feminine, but they both possessed that look of stubborn determination about the mouth and chin.

A few kilometres from the city, Bernard turned off the M1 and some metres further he parked the car in front of a roadhouse which was open for business. The flight from Louisville had not been such an ordeal after all, Olivia realised a few minutes later, but sitting opposite him with the narrow width of the table between them was a different matter entirely. He was all at once too large and overpowering, his dark gaze too disturbing, and her relief was indescribably brief when the waiter handed them each a menu to scrutinise.

'Steak and eggs for me,' he said finally, meeting her wary glance across the menu. 'And you, Olivia?'

'A slice of toast and coffee would do, thank you,' she replied, returning the menu reluctantly to the waiter who wrote down their order and departed.

'No wonder you never grew much as a little girl if you can survive on toast and coffee,' Bernard mocked.

'That has nothing to do with my size,' she protested. 'My Aunt Georgina was just as small and, according to her, my mother was the same.'

'Did your aunt have a family of her own?'

Olivia lowered her lashes to avoid his intense scrutiny. 'My aunt wasn't married.'

'Have you no other family?' he persisted, and she felt her back stiffen in protest.

'None.'

As if sensing her withdrawal, Bernard made no further comment and they lapsed into an uncomfortable silence until their breakfast was served.

'What made you give up your job as a librarian to take on something like a bookshop?' Bernard continued his questioning when he eventually pushed his empty plate aside and sugared his coffee.

'Does there have to be a reason?' Olivia sighed, disliking the way he was probing into her personal life.

'There must be a reason for someone like yourself to give up a job in the city to go to a quiet place like Louisville,' he remarked, his glance sharpening. 'Was there someone you wanted to get away from?'

'No.'

'No entanglement of some sort?' he demanded, raising a mocking eyebrow. 'An affair, perhaps?'

'Certainly not!' she gasped with angry indignation. 'The idea is preposterous!'

'Why?' His glance slid over her with a certain familiarity that sent the colour surging into her cheeks. 'You're attractive, you're twenty-six, so Frances tells me, and I refuse to believe you've reached that age without having at least experienced one serious love affair.'

Anger continued to stir deep down inside her as she raised her chin with a touch of defiance. 'Is that what you want to believe?'

'No,' he said calmly, his lips twisting into a semblance of a smile as he leaned back in his seat and observed her through narrowed eyes. 'Crawl out of that shell of yours, Olivia, and don't let me drag everything out of you.'

'Why must you know all there is to know about me?'

'Perhaps it's your reluctance to talk about yourself that makes me curious,' he said, leaning forward suddenly and placing his hand over hers on the table. 'If you don't tell me, I shall go on being curious, and continue to question you.'

The tingling sensation that started in her hand, rose up the length of her arm, and she suppressed a shiver of dislike as she slipped her hand from beneath his and clenched it in her lap. An awkward silence hovered between them until she finally relented and told him what he wanted to know.

'Well, I suppose this will sound silly to you, but—I love books, and I always had a secret desire to have a bookshop of my own. When my aunt died and left me some money, I made my dream come true.'

'So you stuck a pin in the map and that's how you came to Louisville,' he teased, and she felt her anger and tension subside as an involuntary smile quivered on her lips.

'Not quite,' she shook her head. 'I spent a week at the Haskins Motel and Mineral Baths during June this year, and that's how I learnt of the shop that was for sale. With the flat above it, it was ideal.'

'So you bought it, came back to Johannesburg to give up your job, and finally settled in Louisville.'

'Not entirely in that order, but yes, I did,' she nodded, her lips curving into a smile that found no response in him.

'You could have opened up a shop in Johannesburg,' he argued calmly.

'No.' She lowered her glance, but was forced to meet his compelling gaze once more. 'I wanted to get away from the city. Oh, not for the reasons you're thinking of,' she added hastily when she caught a glimpse of mockery in his eyes. 'But because I wanted to go somewhere where people still cared about each other, instead of——'

'Instead of?' he prompted enigmatically when she broke off abruptly, and she wondered whether he would understand. 'Instead of what?' he insisted.

'Do you know that I sat in a bus once in Johannesburg and watched a woman being beaten and robbed without anyone lifting a finger to help her?' she said eventually, her glance unconsciously pleading. 'Imagine that same scene in Louisville's main street, and tell me whether you think everyone would just pass by and let it happen?'

His lips tightened perceptibly as he said tersely, 'You've made your point.'

They finished their coffee in silence before Bernard paid the bill and drove her directly to the estate agent's offices.

'Wait here for me,' he said as he double-parked and leaned across her to open her door. 'What I have to do won't take longer than an hour, then I'll take you to that place where Vivien usually has her tapestries framed.'

'That's very kind of you, but——'

'No buts,' he interrupted sternly, giving her a gentle push to help her from the car before they held up the traffic. 'See you later.'

Olivia stared after him with a frown settling between her brows. She only hoped he did not intend to tag along wherever she went that morning, or she would never be able to do the personal shopping she had looked forward to. Suppressing a sigh of irritation, she entered the large grey building and took the lift up to the second floor. Mr Roberts could not see her at once and, not wanting to keep Bernard waiting, she glanced repeatedly at the electric clock against the wall. A tense half hour passed before she was shown into the large, panelled office, and within less than twenty minutes the transaction was completed. Olivia made her way down in the lift with a strange sense of loss. She could not possibly have kept the house, and yet she was finding it now so desperately hard to part with it. It had been the only home she had ever known, and now it was no longer hers.

Bernard arrived moments after she had stepped out on to the pavement, and she hurriedly climbed into the car beside him.

'Have you been waiting long?' he asked, steering the car expertly into the traffic.

'No, I've only just come out of there.'

'I think we'll have tea first, don't you?'

It was a statement, not a question, and Olivia heard herself say meekly, 'If you say so.'

Bernard parked the car in a side-street eventually, and they walked the short distance to the tea room where he ordered tea and scones despite her protests. She was not in the least hungry, but, when their order arrived, Bernard's stern glance told her that, whether she was hungry or not, the scones had to be eaten.

'Do you have to see the agent again?' Bernard asked conversationally when the scones and the tea had finally been dispensed with.

'No,' she shook her head, veiling her eyes. 'The papers have been signed, and the sale has been completed.'

'So you've broken the final tie with Johannesburg.' He put a rough finger on a tender spot, making her wince.

'I suppose you could put it that way, yes.'

'Any regrets?'

'No regrets, only ...' Her voice trailed off into silence as she swallowed down the lump which had risen in her throat. 'I grew up in that house, and I have some very happy memories of the years I spent there.'

Bernard studied her closely for some time before he said quite firmly, 'You're going to be much happier at Louisville.'

'You sound as though you're very certain of that,' she remarked, pulling herself together with an effort.

'It's inevitable,' he shrugged his broad shoulders. 'You'll get married one of these days, and——'

'Oh, no,' she interrupted swiftly, her heartbeats quickening in protest. 'I don't think I——'

'You're not planning on becoming a spinster like your aunt, are you?' he demanded, his incredulous glance sweeping over her.

'No,' she shifted uncomfortably beneath his gaze. 'It doesn't pay always to plan the future down to the last detail.'

His lips twitched slightly, indicating some inner amusement that merely served to anger her. 'Then you do plan to marry some day?'

'If and when I meet the right man, yes,' she replied stiffly.

His eyes darkened perceptibly, but he said nothing as

he rose to pay for their tea and guided her from the tea room.

The firm Vivien had mentioned, which took care of the framing of the tapestries, was a little out of the city, but Bernard seemed in no hurry to get Olivia there although the traffic had thinned out considerably. When he finally parked the Mercedes in the parking area in front of a white-washed building, she was surprised to see him climb out with her, accompanying her across the flagged path towards the entrance.

'Do you have any idea what kind of frame Vivien would want?' she was forced to ask once they had entered the building.

'Vivien usually leaves the choice to the discretion of the framers,' he answered abruptly, and Olivia had the distinct impression that he was angry with her for some reason.

Well, let him be angry, she thought miserably. His probing questions had infuriated her more than once during the past few hours, and if her replies were not to his satisfaction then she couldn't care less what he thought.

'I'm at your disposal for the rest of the day, so just say where you want to go, and I'll take you,' he said as they stepped into the sunshine once more and walked across to his hired car.

'Please, Mr King ... Bernard,' she corrected when his dark glance chastised her. 'There's really no need for you to drive me all over the place. If you'd drop me off at the news agency then we could perhaps meet each other somewhere in town for lunch, or——'

His large hand gripped her arm and silenced her more effectively than words could have done. 'Must you always protest so much, Olivia?'

'You surely have things to do, and I——'

'I've done all I came to do.'

'Oh!'

Her startled expression became mutinous as he assisted

her into the car and walked round to his side. Was he so thick-skinned that he could not see that she wanted some time alone in Johannesburg to do some personal shopping? Or was he accustomed to Ilona dragging him all over the place when she required a new wardrobe? Olivia shook herself mentally. Somehow she just could not imagine someone as overpoweringly masculine as Bernard King sitting about in a ladies' dress shop while Ilona made her purchases.

'Do you find my company distasteful?' he asked with a directness that was disconcerting as he slid his arm along the back of the seat and turned to face her before he started the car, and the warm masculine scent of his body so close to hers attacked her senses in a way that made her recoil from him inwardly.

'No!' she almost choked on the denial. 'No, of course not. It's just that——'

'You don't like being an inconvenience, I know,' he replied for her quite incorrectly. 'Well, you're *not* inconveniencing me, and I *have* nothing else to do, so let's stop this senseless argument and tell me where you want to go.

Olivia kept her eyes riveted to her hands in her lap. She could tell him, of course, that she needed to purchase a few items of clothing, but how embarrassing if he should insist on coming with her. She had no specific shop in mind, and had intended browsing through several until she found what she wanted, but, with Bernard intending to play chauffeur, it was out of the question. She relented eventually, giving him the address of the news agency she had to call on, and deciding, with angry reluctance, that her shopping spree would have to be postponed indefinitely.

To her relief, Bernard moved away from her and started the car in silence, and when they finally reached their destination, he would once again not allow her to enter the building on her own. She was forced to suffer his presence while she collected the books which the news agency still had in stock and handed over a list of titles which they told her would have to be ordered specially, but there was not a moment that she was not aware of that tall, bulky figure standing silently beside her, listening, watching, and appraising her with those dark, inscrutable eyes of his.

'Where to now?' he wanted to know when they were seated in the car once more, and Olivia felt her nerves being stretched to a point where she could no longer think straight.

'I ... there's nothing else I have to do,' she said helplessly.

His eyebrows rose incredulously. 'No friends you want to look up either?'

'No.'

'Lost contact with them so soon?' he demanded mockingly. 'Or is it that you don't want me to meet them?'

Olivia's anger flared sharply. 'If you must know, I haven't any friends to look up.'

'No friends?' he mocked, turning towards her. 'But surely——'

'The friends I had at university are all married with families of their own,' she admitted reluctantly. 'We drifted apart years ago.'

Bernard stared at her down-bent head for some time with an enigmatic expression in his eyes before he turned away and started the car, backing it out of the parking area and swerving it into the stream of oncoming traffic.

'Where are we going?' she asked tentatively after he had made several turnings through the centre of the bustling city with its tall buildings towering above them and casting shadows across the busy street.

'I made arrangements for us to lunch at a hotel,' he told her with harsh abruptness. 'We have an hour to kill, so we might as well go there now, freshen up, and have a leisurely drink before we eat.'

Olivia accepted this in silence, an uneasy silence that

lingered until, after washing her hands and checking on her appearance in the hotel cloakroom, she joined him in the lounge. Except for a few other people seated at the far end of the large room, they were alone and quite secluded behind the large stand of potted plants, she noticed, lowering herself into the cool leather armchair opposite him with the small, round table between them. He ordered a beer for himself, and a sherry for her, and Olivia welcomed the intrusion into the tense atmosphere that hovered between them when the steward arrived with their order.

She sipped at her drink and the liquid seemed to flow through her veins, steadying her quivering nerves and allowing her a measure of calmness in the presence of this brooding, silent man who seemed bent upon making her feel as uncomfortable as possible by his intense scrutiny.

'Isn't the sherry to your liking?' he asked finally, his deep voice sending shivers up her spine.

'It's fine, thank you.'

'Then why were you frowning?'

'Was I frowning?' she prevaricated, meeting his glance over the rim of her glass.

'Olivia,' he sighed heavily, his lips tightening with a touch of impatience. 'Stop answering my questions with another question. You know you were frowning, and I want to know why.'

She observed him for a moment from beneath lowered lashes, her glance lingering on the strong jaw, the firm mouth, and the slight paleness of his cheeks which had been covered by a beard only a few days ago, and she realised, almost with regret, that she would not be able to think of him again as the 'Bearded Monster'.

'You look different without your beard,' she said without thinking, but she could have bitten her tongue off when she noticed the glint of mockery in the depths of his eyes.

'Would you say that shaving it off has improved by appearance?' he wanted know, fingering his jaw, and obviously finding some amusement in the flush that stole into her cheeks.

'I suppose you could say that, yes,' she replied evasively, raising her glass to her lips and swallowing down a mouthful of sherry to hide her confusion.

'That doesn't sound very encouraging,' he mocked her ruthlessly.

Olivia lowered her glance to the glass which she clenched so tightly between her fingers. 'My opinion doesn't really matter.'

'I'm *asking* for your opinion.'

The situation was suddenly not without humour, and she felt a smile tugging at the corners of her mouth as she looked up and met his eyes unwaveringly. 'Well, it ... you don't look so ferocious any more.'

'Did I look ferocious?' he smiled suddenly.

'Yes,' she admitted, laughing nervously. 'You scared me to death that day when you walked into my shop for the first time.'

'I know,' he nodded, draining his glass of beer.

'You know?'

'Yes,' he replied solemnly, but devilment lurked in his eyes. 'You were shaking so much I could hear your bones rattling.'

'That's not true!' she gasped, and then she surprised even herself as she heard the laughter bubble past her lips.

'Do you know that's the first time I've heard you laugh? Really laugh, I mean?' he remarked soberly, a peculiar, most unfathomable expression flitting across his face, and her smile froze as she felt a tremor shake through her.

Carefully avoiding his glance, Olivia drained her glass and placed it on the table before her. 'Isn't it time we went in to lunch?'

'Isn't it time you relaxed a little and stopped being so tensed up?' he counter-questioned, rising to his feet and taking her arm as they went through to the dining-room.

The flight back to Louisville that afternoon was not as smooth as their early morning flight to Johannesburg. The wind had come up and it buffeted the small plane relentlessly, but it subsided gradually as they approached the tropical climate of the northern Transvaal.

'Louisville isn't far now,' Bernard remarked eventually, glancing at his wristwatch. 'Another fifteen minutes and we'll most probably be there.'

'I'm glad.'

'Tired?' he asked, glancing at her quickly.

'Not particularly,' she replied drowsily, leaning back in her seat and allowing her thoughts to linger on the events of that day.

'Glad to get away from me, then?'

'I never said that,' she contradicted swiftly when she noticed the tightening of his lips.

'No, you didn't, did you?' he agreed, but the atmosphere was all at once unbearably tense again.

They landed on Bernard's private runway fifteen minutes later as he had predicted, and Olivia's legs were decidedly wobbly as they walked the short distance to the Land Rover, but Bernard's steadying hand was beneath her elbow, tightening instantly when she tripped over a loose stone on the uneven ground.

After a day in Johannesburg, where the days were still relatively cool, the late afternoon heat of the bushveld made her feel as though she had walked into a furnace, and she was thankful even for the warm breeze that brushed across her face through the open windows of the Land Rover as they drove towards the house, for it at least made some attempt to cool her.

Bernard parked the Land Rover beneath a shady tree and Olivia was all at once in a hurry to get back to her own peaceful surroundings when she found herself standing in front of him on the gravel driveway.

'Thank you very much for——'

'You're not going yet,' he told her firmly, his fingers latching on to her slender wrist as he drew her towards the house. 'I can do with a long, cool drink, and I hate drinking alone.'

'I really must——'

'You really must have a drink with me, Olivia,' he interrupted again, his touch burning her skin as he led her on to the verandah.

A few minutes later Olivia found herself seated with a cool orange drink in her hand, while she watched Bernard drink deeply on his cold beer. The shadows lengthened and deepened across the evergreen lawns as she watched the sun which was fast becoming a red ball of fire in the west, its rays having a magical effect on the rugged mountains as it changed the rock-like formations from drab brown to bright amber.

'You must have a beautiful view of the sunset from here,' she sighed involuntarily, her glance lingering on the scene spread out before her, and losing herself momentarily in the silence of the veld.

'If you stay to dinner you could watch it with me,' he suggested, stretching his long legs out before him, but Olivia was instantly filled with alarm at the prospect of sharing yet another meal with him.

'No, I—I really must go now. There's so much I still want to do this evening.'

'Will you stay to dinner another evening?' he persisted as she placed her empty glass on the tray and rose to her feet.

'Perhaps,' she agreed hesitantly, but her reply appeared to satisfy him, for he got to his feet and walked with her towards her Apache. 'Thank you for taking me with you. I really am grateful,' she said, extending her hand towards him. 'Goodbye.'

'Not "goodbye", Olivia,' he contradicted with a peculiar little smile on his lips as he enveloped her hand in his and tightened his grip when she would have withdrawn hers. 'Just *tot siens*, till we meet again, and that will be soon, I hope.'

'Not if I can help it,' she thought distractedly, freeing herself at last and escaping in her car. This was the last time she would allow Vivien to inveigle her into something which would involve being alone with Bernard in some way. Never again did she want to live through another day such as the one she had just experienced. Bernard King was much too disturbing, and far too detestable at times when he insisted on probing into her affairs. He had dominated almost every minute of her time in Johannesburg, brushing aside her resistance as one would brush aside an irritating fly, and nothing she had planned ever came to fruition.

He was overbearing and arrogant, but she had to admit to herself that he had been quite pleasant company when she had allowed herself to relax on a few occasions. He had somehow turned the flight, which had been nerve-racking at first, into an adventure she would remember for some time to come, and when he was not mocking her, or probing into her private life, she had found his strong, forceful presence a comfort. He was not as frightening as she had originally imagined him to be, and beneath that hard exterior she sensed a warm, friendly nature that could very easily attract her in an unguarded moment.

Startled and angered at the trend of her thoughts, she shook herself free and concentrated on the road ahead. Bernard King was not at all her type of man, and the less she saw of him, the better for her shattered peace of mind.

CHAPTER SEVEN

THERE had barely been enough time for Olivia to hang up her bunch of keys the following morning before Ilona Haskins walked into her shop. Her amber linen dress looked cool and elegant, Olivia thought as she looked up with her usual smile, but the answering smile on Ilona's lips never reached those beautiful, long-lashed eyes as they surveyed Olivia with deliberate coolness.

'Bernard tells me you had quite a pleasant trip to Johannesburg yesterday, although he found it quite amusing having a novice such as yourself in the plane with him,' that deceptively warm, silky voice fired the first shot and found its mark with an accuracy that made Olivia wince inwardly.

'No doubt he did find me an amusing novice.'

'I'm so glad he took my advice at last and shaved that dreadful beard off,' Ilona continued chattily, but her watchful eyes never left Olivia's face. 'He's so much more attractive without it, don't you think?'

'I suppose so, yes,' Olivia agreed guardedly, wondering confusedly were this conversation would lead to.

'But of course he is, and you know it,' Ilona insisted, her expression hardening. 'I must warn you, though. Bernard is a terrible tease, so don't take him too seriously, will you?'

Olivia stiffened instantly. 'Miss Haskins, what exactly are you trying to say?'

Those lovely arched eyebrows rose imperiously. 'Do you need me to spell it out for you?'

'I wish you would,' Olivia stated calmly, but there was nothing calm about the way her insides were beginning to shake.

'Very well, then,' Ilona began, no longer attempting to hide her feelings behind a façade of friendliness. 'Don't get any romantic notions about Bernard, because you might as well know that he and I have had an understanding—an intimate understanding—for some years now.'

'You're mistaken, Miss Haskins,' Olivia protested adamantly, her face growing hot and cold. 'I have no interest whatsoever in Bernard King, so you need have no fear as far as I'm concerned.'

Ilona's lips twisted cynically as she added the final touch to her accusation. 'One wouldn't say so, judging by the way you've been chasing after him lately.'

'How dare you!'

Hurt and angered by the unfairness of Ilona's accusation, Olivia gripped the edge of the counter until her knuckles showed white through her faintly tanned skin, but she shrank inwardly from the look of intense hatred in Ilona's eyes as she said:

'I dare, Miss Logan, because I've given up six years of my life for Bernard, and I don't intend to lose him now to an insignificant little shopkeeper such as yourself.'

Without another word, Ilona marched out of the shop, almost colliding with Vivien who was about to enter. They exchanged a hasty greeting, but Ilona did not linger as she made her way across the street to where her Triumph was parked.

'She seemed to be in a hurry to leave,' Vivien remarked, staring thoughtfully at Ilona's taut, retreating figure before she turned to face Olivia who stood pale and shaking behind the counter. Her eyes narrowed perceptibly. 'Is there something the matter, Olivia?'

Olivia was not sure whether she ought to laugh or cry, but instead she made a visible effort to pull herself together as she heard herself stammer, 'No, of—of course not.'

'Has Ilona said something to upset you?'

'No, no!'

'Of course she has,' Vivien insisted, her narrowed glance

watching the colour fluctuate in Olivia's cheeks. 'It was about yesterday's trip to Johannesburg, wasn't it?'

The accuracy of her guess made Olivia look away hastily to hide her revealing expression. 'Vivien, I'd rather not discuss it.'

'Well, I do!' Vivien persisted, coming round to the other side of the counter and forcing Olivia to face her. 'Did she tell you to keep off the grass, so to speak?'

Olivia stared into those probing dark eyes so like Bernard's and knew it would be useless offering a denial. 'More or less, yes,' she admitted feebly.

Vivien gestured angrily. 'Don't take any notice of what she said, my dear.'

'Oh, Vivien, let's talk about something else,' Olivia sighed, finding it increasingly difficult to understand why Ilona should have considered her a threat as far as the relationship between Bernard and herself was concerned. Good heavens, she hardly knew the man, and there never could be anything between them other than a mutual interest in Frances. Shaking herself free of these thoughts, she forced a smile to her unwilling lips as she faced Vivien. 'Did you manage here in the shop yesterday?'

'I managed perfectly,' Vivien smiled warmly. 'I just hope you found everything in order this morning.'

'Everything seems to be in wonderful order,' Olivia assured her. 'Everything except my shattered nerves,' she thought, a little warmth beginning to flow through her veins.

'I enjoyed myself so much that I wouldn't mind helping out if you ever need to go away again,' Vivien continued enthusiastically, and Olivia could have hugged her for saying so.

'You're very kind, Vivien.'

'I'm serious, you know,' Vivien insisted, her quick smile harbouring a hint of humour. 'If you ever need an assistant, I'm available.'

'I'll remember that,' Olivia agreed with a brief laugh.

'What was *your* day like yesterday?' Vivien asked suddenly, and Olivia tensed inwardly.

'Pleasant, thank you,' she replied politely, changing the subject hastily. 'Our tapestries should be ready within a month.'

'Oh, good,' Vivien enthused.

She remained a few minutes longer, discussing what had occurred in the shop the day before, but when she finally left Olivia felt depressed and more than a little angry as she recalled the conversation she had had with Ilona.

So Bernard had found her an amusing passenger, a novice, and no doubt he and Ilona had discussed this at great length the previous evening. She could accept this, for it was the truth; she *had* been nervous to a certain extent. But to claim that she was chasing Bernard King was more than just a misrepresentation of the truth, it was a downright lie! This unworthy accusation could only stem from Ilona's own insecurity with regard to Bernard's affections, Olivia decided, pitying that lovely creature who looked upon every other unattached woman as an adversary. 'If only Ilona knew how little interest I have in Bernard,' Olivia thought, a wry smile lifting the corners of her mouth, but the smile was gone the next instant as a sobering thought pressed to the fore. What if Bernard King himself considered she had been chasing after him?

'No, he couldn't!' Olivia thought wildly. No one knew better than he that Vivien had engineered the entire situation, or did he perhaps think that she had prompted Vivien privately? 'Oh, lord!' she moaned, burying her face in her hands for a moment, but the sound of footsteps crossing her threshold made her pull herself together sharply.

Olivia found it difficult to shake off her disturbing thoughts, but she somehow managed to get through the rest of the day without letting it trouble her too much. She could not, however, prevent the sigh of relief from escaping past her lips when it was time to lock up the shop for the night, but, turning to take her bunch of keys off the hook behind the counter, she had the most peculiar sensation that she was no longer alone.

'Good afternoon, Olivia.'

'Oh!' She swung round in alarm to find Bernard standing framed in the entrance, dressed in a light grey safari suit, expensive suede shoes, and the inevitable wide-brimmed hat dangling from his hand. 'Good afternoon,' she greeted him nervously.

He lowered his glance to the keys in her hands. 'Are you about to close up the shop?'

'Yes.'

'Good, then I'll come up and have a cup of coffee with you,' he stated quite calmly, but Olivia felt her heart quicken with something close to fear.

'Do—do you think that's wise?' she asked unsteadily, unable to meet the intensity of his gaze.

'I'm not afraid that you will put arsenic in my coffee, if that's what you mean,' the deep mockery in his voice scraped along her sensitive nerves.

'No, that's not what I meant,' she corrected with a calmness she was far from experiencing, for she had only one desire, and that was to get rid of him as quickly as possible before Ilona found him there. 'I was thinking of what people would say if they saw your Land Rover outside my shop after hours,' she said at last.

'I couldn't care less about what people say,' Bernard exploded with a harshness that made her flinch. 'If you don't feel inclined to offer me something to drink, then say so and I'll go.'

Ufezela the scorpion had reared its tail to deliver its deadly sting, and Olivia felt a shiver of apprehension and fear make its way along her spine. The situation was suddenly dangerous, leaving her no safe alternative to grasp at.

'I'm sorry,' she said at last, sealing her own fate. 'I—I

didn't mean to sound so inhospitable. You—you're welcome to come up and have coffee with me.'

Bernard accepted this with a brief nod and followed her from the shop in silence, but Olivia felt as though every nerve in her body was screaming for release. After accepting his hospitality, and that of his sister, how could she refuse him, but there was Ilona to reckon with, and the dreadful accusations she had made only that morning. Heaven knew she had no desire to entertain him in her flat, but would Ilona see it as such?

Her hands were unsteady as she unlocked the door to her flat and led the way inside. Her small lounge seemed to shrink somehow in size the moment he entered it, and Olivia gestured nervously that he should sit down.

'Don't you find it rather small?' he asked, almost reading her thoughts as he lowered himself into the nearest easy chair and glanced about him with obvious interest.

Olivia was instantly on the defensive. 'It's quite big enough for me, considering I have to do all the chores myself.'

'I wasn't criticising.'

His glance clashed with hers and she was overwhelmed by a sudden fierce guilt. 'I'm sorry, I thought for a moment——' She caught her lip between her teeth and turned away. 'I'll go and put the kettle on.'

The simple task of making coffee restored her composure to a certain extent, but with every fibre of her being she was conscious of Bernard's disturbing presence in the adjoining room, and nature had participated in the fact that Bernard King would not be the kind of man one could overlook with ease. He was far too forceful; too dominant, and much too large not to stand out even in a crowd. Ufezela the scorpion; deceptively placid when not disturbed, but deadly when roused. Olivia shivered at the thought and carried the tray of coffee through to the lounge where he sat waiting, relaxed and uncaring with his long, muscular legs stretched out before him.

'I meant to ask,' he said after a while. 'Did you enjoy your first taste of flying yesterday?'

'Very much,' Olivia replied with polite coolness, unable to prevent herself from adding, 'Despite the fact that my being a novice at it apparently amused you so much.'

'What the devil are you talking about?' His cup went down into the saucer with a clatter that made her jump. 'You were nervous, and that was understandable, but I never found it amusing.'

Olivia stared at him in confused silence. Was it possible that Ilona could have lied, or was Bernard's almost aggressive attitude a cover-up for a guilty conscience?

'I supposed you preferred carrying passengers who've had some flying experience,' she said nervously, trying to give a reasonable explanation for her remark without involving Ilona.

'I don't particularly care who flies with me, just as long as they don't go crazy and grab at the controls,' he contradicted sternly, and for some reason she could not explain, she was convinced that he was speaking the truth. How much, then, could she believe of what Ilona had said? 'You make a good cup of coffee, Olivia,' Bernard interrupted her confused thoughts.

'Thank you,' she murmured, avoiding his eyes. *If only he would go*, she kept thinking, still smarting inwardly from Ilona's unfair accusations early that morning.

'You seem agitated about something.'

Olivia's lashes flew upwards in startled surprise, a denial tripping almost frantically from her lips. 'I'm not agitated about anything.'

'Then you're afraid of something,' he insisted, his expression hardening, his eyes searching.

'Don't be silly!'

He was beside her suddenly on the sofa, removing the cup from her nerveless fingers and taking her hands in his before she could so much as utter a protest. 'Your hands are cold and shaking. You're not ill, are you?'

'I'm perfectly all right, thank you,' she choked out the words, frightened now by his nearness and his touch, and the burning intensity of his eyes as they raked over her, taking in the swift and agitated rise and fall of her breast as her breath quickened.

'Perhaps you should let Peter give you a check-up.'

'Bernard, please! There's nothing the matter with me physically,' she pleaded, dragging her hands from his and edging further away from him. 'I think I may have turned the air-conditioner up too high. I'm cold, that's all.'

'I think you should see Peter at any rate,' Bernard persisted, and to her horror he walked across to the telephone and lifted the receiver. 'This bushveld heat can have strange effects on someone who isn't used to it.'

Olivia was beside him in an instant, placing a restraining hand on his arm and finding it a peculiar sensation to feel the soft, dark hair beneath her fingertips, and the warm, hard muscles tightening beneath her grip. He looked down at her small hand, so pale against his tanned arm, and a peculiar expression crept into his eyes.

Snatching her hand away almost at once as her cheeks flamed, she protested weakly, 'You'll be wasting Peter's time. I don't need a doctor.'

His eyes flickered strangely as they met hers. 'Are you sure?'

'Yes—yes, I'm sure,' she insisted, the tension stretching to breaking point between them.

'Well, I must be on my way,' he announced at last and, picking up his hat, he raised it in salute. 'Thanks for the coffee, Olivia.'

As the door closed behind him she collapsed into the chair beside the telephone, a trembling hand at her throat where the aching muscles stood out prominently. She could not have stood another minute of his company, she told herself as she gently massaged her throat. Did he not realise that his presence there in her flat would upset Ilona, or was he deliberately trying to make the poor woman jealous?

'Oh, lord, I wish he wouldn't drag me into his plans,' she groaned to herself as her nerves settled back into their rightful order.

After experiencing two traumatic days the rest of the week seemed to slip by in its usual leisurely fashion, but Olivia was in for a rude awakening the Thursday afternoon when she looked up to find Bernard standing on the other side of the counter, dressed this time in pale grey slacks and spotless white shirt. His dark hair, flecked so abundantly with grey, was brushed back severely from the broad forehead, and his tanned, rugged features spoke of many hours spent in the sun.

'I thought I'd come and find out how you are,' he said without preamble, his probing glance searching for any signs of illness. 'I wondered afterwards if the flight hadn't upset you in some way.'

Her hands fluttered nervously and she lowered them to her sides, clenching them so tightly that her nails bit into her palms. 'The flight didn't upset me at all and, as I told you before, I'm perfectly well.'

Quick, familiar footsteps prevented him from saying anything further and they both turned to see Vivien approaching with a cake tin in her hands.

'I'm surprised to find you in town in the middle of the week, Bernard?' she smiled up at him with that easy familiarity which Olivia almost envied.

'I had a few things to do in town which couldn't wait.'

'Well, I didn't feel like spending the hours alone at home this afternoon, so I decided to come and have tea with you, Olivia. I've brought along a cake as well,' she added, glancing expectantly at her brother. 'Are you staying to have tea with us, Bernard?'

Olivia groaned silently, but to her relief Bernard said:

'No, I must go, but I think I'll ask Evalina to bake an apple tart for Saturday morning, then I'll come and have tea with Olivia and Frances.'

Subsiding helplessly on to the stool behind the counter, Olivia watched him walk from the shop with those long, firm strides she was beginning to know so well.

'I'm so glad to see he's shaved his beard off,' Vivien remarked, her eyes glowing with an inner satisfaction that puzzled Olivia. 'After six years of having to put up with his hairy face it makes quite a change,' she continued, tilting her head in thought. 'Isn't it strange? It was only Saturday that we were discussing that awful beard of his.'

'Yes, so it was,' Olivia agreed distractedly.

'He looks devilishly handsome without it, doesn't he?'

Olivia avoided Vivien's mischievous glance and evaded the question smartly. 'There's a very strong resemblance between the two of you that I didn't quite notice before.'

Vivien looked at her strangely with a quiet sort of smile hovering about her lips, but Olivia had had enough and went through to the back to put on the kettle.

When the door-bell chimed in her flat that evening, Olivia went cold with fright, but glancing out of her window down into the street below, she assured herself that it was not Bernard before she crossed the lounge and opened the door.

'Tante Maria!' she exclaimed with relief when she saw the plump, motherly figure on her doorstep. 'Do come in, please.'

'We haven't seen much of you these past few days,' the older woman complained. 'So I thought I'd come round and see if you were all right.'

'I'm fine, Tante Maria,' Olivia assured her, but a persistent little voice inside her whispered 'Liar'. 'Sit down and I'll make us a cup of coffee,' Olivia suggested, silencing that little voice quite firmly.

'I noticed that, since you flew to Johannesburg with

Bernard King on Monday, he's called twice to see you,' Tante Maria remarked teasingly some time later as they sat drinking their coffee.

Olivia nodded silently, wondering helplessly whether it would help at all to discuss these new and terrifying problems with this woman she had come to look upon as her friend and confidant.

'He's shaved his beard off, too, I see,' Tante Maria continued, a twinkle of mischief in her blue eyes.

'That beard!' Olivia thought furiously. Everyone seemed to talk about it as if there was something significant about his shaving the darned thing off. Was Bernard King so important in this community that every action, every word had to be discussed and speculated upon?

'Tante Maria ...' She bit her lip nervously, hesitating with indecision before she said: 'Tante, I'm so glad you came this evening, I—I need some advice badly.'

'What is it, my child?' Tante Maria asked with concern. 'If I can help you in any way, then just say so.'

'I ... had another visitor this week,' Olivia said hesitantly. 'Ilona Haskins.'

'Oh?'

Olivia looked away from the older woman's enquiring glance as she felt her cheeks redden with renewed embarrassment. 'She—she made it quite clear that there was an understanding between Bernard and herself, and—and she accused me of chasing after him.'

Tante Maria gestured angrily. 'You shouldn't take any notice of her, child. She's just jealous, that's all. And, as far as accusing you of chasing after him,' she raised her eyes towards the ceiling in a gesture of disgust, 'what does she think she's been doing these past six years?'

'Tante Maria, I have no intention of interfering in whatever relationship there exists between them,' Olivia said with deep sincerity. 'I'm not interested in Bernard King, but he's called twice this week since Ilona came to see me, and I just don't know how to tell him it would be better if he stayed away.'

'Why should you want to do that?' Tante Maria demanded in shocked dismay. 'I'm beginning to think that if he'd wanted to marry Ilona he would have done so years ago, but if he's showing an interest in you, then why send him away because of Ilona's silly remarks?'

'But I don't want anything to do with him,' Olivia exclaimed desperately, finding it totally ridiculous that Bernard could be even remotely interested in her.

'You're fond of his daughter, though,' Tante Maria reminded her thoughtfully.

'Yes, I am,' Olivia nodded, 'but that doesn't mean I have to be fond of him as well.'

Tante Maria's glance held a hint of humour that found no echo in Olivia as she heard the older woman say, 'He's very wealthy, and would make an excellent husband.'

'Tante Maria, I'm not looking for a husband, and wealth has never attracted me. Besides ...' she drew a quivering, frightened breath, 'I think you're quite mistaken about him having any real interest in me.'

'Then tell me, Olivia,' Tante Maria began earnestly as she leaned forward in her chair with an expression on her face that made Olivia hold her breath. 'Why would a man like Bernard King suddenly shave off a beard he's had for so many years, and why would he come to town twice in the middle of the week, all dressed up, when for years he's only been seen on Saturdays like most of the other ranchers in the district?'

If a stick of dynamite had exploded at her feet Olivia could not have been more stunned and shocked as she expelled the air from her lungs and shrank deeper into her chair, her grey eyes wide and frightened. 'Tante Maria ... I hope you're mistaken,' she whispered shakily.

'Perhaps,' the older woman shrugged without a glimmer of a smile on her face, 'but it looks that way to me.'

'Oh, heavens!' Olivia's heart hammered in her throat as she covered her flaming face with trembling hands. This was dreadful! Tante Maria had to be mistaken, but her explanation sounded so frighteningly logical that Olivia shivered as if someone had dropped a block of ice down her back, and her face, when she finally lowered her hands, was pale and pinched, her eyes a deep blue instead of grey. 'What am I going to do?' she pleaded on a note of desperation.

'Nothing,' Tante Maria replied instantly, her expression stating clearly that, had she been Olivia's age, she would have been thrilled at the knowledge that someone such as Bernard King should be interested in her, and she was obviously finding Olivia's reluctance difficult to understand. 'Ignore what Ilona said to you, and let Bernard King come and see you if he wants to.'

'But I don't particularly want to see *him*!'

'You can't be rude to a member of the King family,' Tante Maria warned her with some severity. 'They're respected and very well liked in this community, Olivia. Remember that.'

Tante Maria left soon afterwards, announcing that she intended getting to bed early, but for Olivia it was the beginning of a long, torturous night with very little sleep as she tossed away the hours until sunrise the following day. She had wanted help and advice from Tante Maria, but their discussion had merely increased her problems a thousand times more. Bernard King interested in her? It was ridiculous, and yet ... Why *did* he shave that infernal beard off? It couldn't have been because of her, but Tante Maria seemed to think so, and Vivien's pointed remarks and satisfied expression now seemed to indicate that she thought so too.

'They're wrong, though,' she spoke aloud into the darkness as she recalled Ilona's remark. 'I'm so glad he took my advice at last and shaved that dreadful beard off.'

That statement contradicted all Tante Maria's claims, but it did nothing to eliminate the growing wariness within Olivia. Bernard King was not the kind of man she could ever become interested in. He was far too disturbing for her ever to relax in his company, and the mere thought of him being interested in her, or wanting to take her in his arms, made her suppress a shudder as she shrank deeper beneath the sheets, almost as if she could escape from her thoughts in that manner.

But what if it were true? Oh, no, no, *no*! She couldn't bear it! And what about Ilona? Ilona who had stated so vehemently that she had given up six years of her life for Bernard and had no intention of losing him to an insignificant little shopkeeper like herself?

Insignificant—that's just what she was. So why should Bernard show any real interest in *her*? There had to be some other, more acceptable explanation. There just *had* to be!

Olivia struggled through the following day, her fear of coming face to face with Bernard making her jumpy each time someone entered the shop, but at the end of the day lack of sleep and the increasing heat took its toll, and she crawled into bed immediately after an early supper, falling asleep instantly and dreamlessly.

When Bernard brought Frances to the shop the following morning, Olivia was relieved to see that he came no further than the door, and merely raised his hand in greeting before climbing back into his Land Rover. Frances stared after him for a moment before hurrying towards Olivia and pressing a cake tin into her hands.

'That's the apple pie Daddy promised you,' she announced when Olivia frowned down at it curiously.

'Oh, yes,' she smiled. 'I'd forgotten.'

'Daddy looks so different without his beard, and I think he looks much nicer too, but Miss Haskins was very angry with him when she came to the farm last Sunday morning and saw that he'd shaved it off,' Frances informed Olivia as they took the cake tin through to the back. 'Don't you like him better without his beard, Olivia?'

'Frances ...' she hesitated confusedly. Ilona had gone to great lengths to make her understand that Bernard had shaved his beard off because she had asked him to, but Frances, without realising it, had just contradicted that statement. 'Why did your father shave his beard off?' she asked at length, afraid, yet determined to get to the bottom of this mystery once and for all.

'I told him you didn't particularly like a beard,' the child announced boldly, and a wave of faintness over-whelmed Olivia, forcing her to clutch at the table for support.

'Oh, Frances, how *could* you!'

'But you *did* say so, Olivia,' Frances reminded her only too vividly of her evasive remark which should not have gone further than this shop, and most certainly should not have been taken seriously.

'Yes, I know, but——' Olivia broke off abruptly at the sight of Frances' anxious little face staring up at her in con-sternation, and hugged the child instead. 'Oh, it doesn't matter.'

But it *did* matter, she thought wildly. Tante Maria had been right after all, it seemed, and heaven only knew how she was going to face Bernard in future, knowing that her innocent remark had been relayed to him and taken seri-ously. Dear heaven, was there no escape from this tangled mess she was finding herself in?

She began to hate the clock against the wall as it ticked the minutes away that morning, bringing her closer to the time when he would join them for tea. The only fact that consoled her in some way was that Frances would be there to ease the inevitable tension, but even that thought offered her little comfort when he eventually strode into the shop, tall, broad, and so very self-possessed.

'Am I too early?' he asked, lowering himself on to the stool beside the counter, and looking as though he had every right to be there.

'I'll go and put the kettle on,' Olivia said in nervous haste, but Frances tugged at her hand and held her back.

'I can do that for you, Olivia,' she offered, disappearing into the back before Olivia could protest.

'She isn't a nuisance, is she?' Bernard wanted to know, gesturing towards Frances' retreating figure with the pig-tails bobbing down her back as she went.

'Not at all,' Olivia assured him, ill at ease in his company and wondering how she would get through the length of his stay without making a complete idiot of herself. 'Frances helps me so much that she's become quite indispensable on a Saturday morning,' she added.

A customer coming into the shop brought a momentary respite, and she excused herself hastily, discovering to her horror that her legs were shaking as she attended to the old lady who wanted a book of crochet patterns. Finding just the right pattern book took a little time, and Olivia finally discovered that not only had Frances put the kettle on, but she had made the tea as well, and Bernard, quite oblivious of the elderly lady's curious glances in his direction, was carrying the tray of tea through to the front of the shop, with Frances close behind him with the apple pie neatly sliced.

He was really the most astonishing man she had ever met, Olivia thought helplessly. He was irritating and in-sufferable, yet at times so absolutely human that it was almost infuriating. Frances chatted gaily while they had their tea, quite unaware of the tension coiling through Olivia as she became increasingly aware of Bernard's specu-lative, searching glances that sent the colour surging into her cheeks on several occasions as she recalled her conversa-tion with Tante Maria. When he finally left, promising to collect Frances at one o'clock, Olivia was trembling so much that she could hardly carry the tray through to the back without rattling the cups in their saucers as she did so. If only Ilona had not flung those hateful accusations at her, and Tante Maria had not voiced those frightening observations, then this encounter with Bernard might have turned into quite a pleasant interlude, but Frances, dear innocent little Frances, had set the ball rolling by disclosing part of their discussion the previous Saturday, and the entire situation had since got out of hand.

'You must thank Evalina for the lovely apple pie,' she told Bernard when he eventually came to collect Frances.

His eyes glinted strangely in the sunlight as he looked down at her from his great height. 'Why don't you come out to Mountain View for lunch and thank her yourself?'

Olivia was instantly on her guard, rejecting his suggestion without further thought. 'I'm afraid I can't, I——'

'Please come, Olivia,' Frances pleaded, adding weight to her father's suggestion, but on this occasion Olivia would not be swayed.

'Another time, perhaps, Frances,' she said gently, running the back of her fingers across one rosy cheek. 'There are so many things I have to do this afternoon that I don't get time for during the week.'

'But it's going to be a whole long week before I see you again,' Frances complained disappointedly.

'A week passes very quickly,' Olivia assured her with a slight smile, but the warmth and tenderness in her glance was unmistakable. 'Before you know it, the week-end will be here again, and we'll have all Saturday morning together again, with a lot of hard work thrown in for good measure.'

'I suppose so,' Frances sighed reluctantly, flinging her arms about Olivia's waist unexpectedly and hugging her before she climbed into the Land Rover.

'I'll see you again soon,' Bernard said, extending his large hand towards her, and Olivia wondered faintly whether this was a promise or a threat as she shook hands with him and watched him walk round to the driver's side.

'A promise or a threat,' she echoed her thoughts with a touch of hysteria. To Bernard it might have been a promise, but to her it was a threat; a threat in the form of Ilona Haskins, and a warning that she would have to take special care in future as far as Bernard King was concerned.

CHAPTER EIGHT

BERNARD came to the shop several times during the following weeks, lingering long enough only to have tea with Olivia before returning to the farm, and on each occasion she felt almost limp with relief after his departure. He brought Frances to the shop on Saturday mornings, but each time, when he returned just before one to fetch her, Olivia had a plausible excuse ready when the inevitable invitation to lunch at Mountain View was extended. Frances, who had become a splendid little assistant, never hid her disappointment, but Bernard's expression invariably become curiously closed, sending shivers of apprehension through Olivia which she had difficulty in explaining to herself.

Her fear of encountering Ilona's wrath once more never eventuated either, for she never put in an appearance again, and Olivia could only surmise that Ilona had considered the one warning enough—which indeed it had been!

As the weeks slipped by into November, Olivia found it almost impossible to believe that more than two months had passed since her arrival in Louisville. Vivien arrived one Tuesday morning with a bouquet of early summer roses from her garden, but, as usual, she did not stay long and, as the hours hastened on towards the afternoon, Olivia began to experience the achingly familiar tension winding its way through her body. It was one of the days in the week when Bernard always paid her a visit, and she found herself glancing up each time a car came down the street, or jumping nervously at the sound of heavy footsteps outside the shop. Then, inexplicably, she experienced a feeling of unwanted concern and disappointment when it was time to lock up for the night and there was still no sign of him.

'Oh, what's the matter with me!' she muttered angrily, admonishing herself as she climbed the stairs to her flat with the vase containing Vivien's roses in her hands. She did not *want* to see him, but what if something awful had happened to him? What if he was lying ill at home with no one to care for him? 'Stop it!' she told herself fiercely. 'He has a bevy of Venda servants who'd be only too willing to dance attendance on Ufezela. At any rate, why should *I* care?'

The door-bell chimed just after seven that evening and Olivia went rigid with fright, experiencing also a flicker of anticipation that infuriated her. It chimed again after a few seconds and, shaking herself free of her motionless state, she went to answer it.

'Gerald!' she exclaimed with unutterable relief when she saw the tall, fair man on her doorstep.

'You looked like a scared rabbit for a moment,' he laughed, looking down at her quizzically. 'Were you expecting someone else?'

'No, not really,' she smiled, unable to understand why she should feel vaguely disappointed as she pulled herself together and opened the door wider. 'Come in, please.'

'How's my favourite girl been lately?' he asked eventually, dropping into a chair and grinning up at her mischievously.

'Fine—just fine,' she replied, wringing her hands nervously. 'I'll make us some coffee.'

It took some minutes for her nerves to settle down, but even as she handed Gerald his cup of coffee, her hand shook visibly.

'What's the matter, Olivia? I've never known you to be this jittery.'

'It's nothing,' she lied, avoiding the curiosity and concern in his green eyes. 'Nothing at all.'

'Perhaps you've been overdoing it a bit lately. It could

also be this sudden heatwave we're experiencing,' Gerald speculated thoughtfully. 'Have you been to see a doctor lately?'

'There's nothing the matter with me, Gerald,' she argued, sipping at her hot coffee and striving for an outward calmness. 'How is Sanet?'

'She's all right, I suppose,' Gerald shrugged carelessly, still not convinced that Olivia was not hiding something from him.

'What do you mean, you suppose?' she persisted, determined to steer the conversation in a different direction.

'Well, I saw her at school today, and she looked all right to me.'

'You ought to be ashamed of yourself,' she rebuked him.

'Why?'

'You're throwing your happiness away.'

'No, I'm not,' Gerald protested seriously. 'For once in my life I'm being sensible.'

'You like her, don't you?'

'Yes, but——'

'If she hadn't come from a wealthy family, would it have made a difference to the way you feel about her?' Olivia interrupted with a display of determination that amazed her.

'If she hadn't been so darned wealthy, I might have——' He broke off sharply, grinning at her over the rim of his cup. 'Don't trick me into saying things I don't want to.'

Olivia sighed exasperatedly. 'Have you ever thought of the possibility that your attitude might be causing her a great deal of unhappiness?'

Gerald was instantly suspicious. 'Has she been talking to you?'

'No,' she shook her head firmly. 'I seldom see her, and then only in the shop, but any fool can see she's unhappy about something.'

'What makes you think that *I'm* the cause of her unhappiness?' he demanded with a guarded expression that was almost comical if the situation had not been so serious.

'I happened to see the way she looked at you once.'

'You could be mistaken.'

Olivia shook her head firmly. 'I've been on the outside looking in for the best part of my life, and facial expressions sometimes say so much more than words.'

A car door slammed in the street below and Olivia's ragged nerves reacted accordingly.

'It sounds as though you're about to receive another visitor,' Gerald observed, draining his cup and placing it with Olivia's in the tray.

'Yes,' she replied shakily, 'and I can guess who it is.'

'Who?' he asked, his eyebrows raised above humorous green eyes as she struggled to steady the tremor in her hands.

'Bernard King.'

Her disclosure and the chime of the door-bell was almost simultaneous and, rising instantly to her feet, she walked jerkily across the room towards the door and opened it.

'Hello, Olivia,' Bernard greeted with that slight smile which nearly always succeeded in unnerving her.

'Good evening,' she said in a voice that sounded cool to her own ears as she stood aside for him to enter, but her heart was hammering out an odd rhythm in her breast. 'You know Gerald Thatcher, don't you?'

'Yes, we've met on several occasions,' Bernard admitted, his expression inscrutable as he extended a large hand towards Gerald, who had risen at his entrance. 'I'm pleased I found you here as well, Gerald,' Bernard continued calmly, lowering himself into a chair and making it appear diminutive because of his enormous bulk. 'It's my sister's birthday this coming Saturday, and I'm having a *braai* out at the farm for her. I've already invited Frances' teacher, Miss ... er ... Pretorius, and I'd like you to be there as well.'

Gerald accepted the invitation to the barbecue enthusiastically, but Olivia wished herself anywhere else but there as Bernard turned suddenly and pinned her down with his glance.

'You'll be there, of course, Olivia.'

It was not an invitation but a command, and she found herself stammering, 'Oh, but I can't, I——'

'Why not?' the question was rapped out like the lash of a whip and she flinched inwardly.

'Nothing,' she murmured helplessly. 'I'll come, of course.'

'I'll bring Sanet Pretorius and Olivia out to the farm in my car,' Gerald offered, easing the tension in the air considerably.

'That's an excellent idea,' Bernard nodded, 'and make it about five in the afternoon.'

A frightening little silence threatened and Olivia rose jerkily to her feet and grabbed the tray. 'I'll make us some fresh coffee.'

'Not for me, Olivia,' Gerald declined, rising to his feet. 'I must go.'

'Must you really?' she asked quickly, panic gripping at her throat and tightening mercilessly as she lowered the tray to the table.

Gerald smiled apologetically. 'I've got a pile of examination papers to wade through before tomorrow and, much as I would like to, I really must go. Goodnight, Mr King,' he added politely, receiving a brief nod in return.

'I'll come to the door with you,' she offered, feeling defeated as she excused herself from Bernard who followed her with hard, watchful eyes. She stopped outside with Gerald and lowered her voice drastically. 'I wish you could have stayed longer.'

'Don't tell me you're afraid of being alone with Bernard King?' Gerald teased in a whisper.

'No, of course I'm not afraid,' she denied instantly, but

in her heart she knew it to be a lie. She *was* afraid of Bernard, and even more afraid of the stranger she was becoming to herself. 'Goodnight, Gerald.'

He squeezed her hand gently before going down to his car, and Olivia sighed heavily as she went inside to face a glowering Bernard.

'Where are you going?' he demanded as she picked up the tray without a word and walked a few paces away from him.

'I'm going to make you a cup of coffee.'

'I'll come with you,' he announced, filling her with alarm as he rose to his feet and towered above her.

'I can manage on my own, thank you,' she protested, backing away from him instantly as her heart began to pound uncomfortably.

'I'll come with you all the same,' he replied, quite unperturbed as he followed her into the kitchen and took up most of the confined space. 'Does Gerald Thatcher come here often?'

'Just occasionally—why?' she wanted to know as she switched on the kettle and set out a cup for him.

'Are you serious about him?'

The question jolted her anger, an anger she had not known she possessed until she had met this infuriating man leaning so nonchalantly against the steel cupboard, watching her with dark eyes that seemed to burn holes right through her.

'Forgive me, but I don't think it's any of your business,' she told him coldly, but the next instant she almost cried out with pain as his hand gripped her arm just above the elbow.

'It *is* my business,' he ground out the words, the unmistakable fury in his eyes sending an involuntary shiver through her slender frame. 'I happen to like you, and I wouldn't want you to be hurt.'

'Gerald is a friend, that's all,' she explained angrily,

fighting back the tears that rose to her eyes, 'and the only thing that's hurting me is your hand on my arm.'

'I'm sorry,' he said, releasing her instantly with an expression close to remorse as he watched the imprint of his fingers become a dark angry red against the soft flesh of her upper arm. 'My God, you bruise easily,' he exploded softly, caressing the mark with gentle fingers and sending inexplicable little shivers through her that quickened her pulse.

'Excuse me, the kettle is boiling,' she muttered, her voice sounding choked as she moved beyond his reach.

Her hand was shaking visibly as she handed him his cup of coffee a few seconds later and watched him help himself to milk and sugar before they returned to the lounge. He was much more than merely disturbing, she decided, allowing her glance to slide from the broad shoulders in the cream safari jacket, down to the narrow hips, and along muscular legs encased in matching pants. He was aggressively masculine, and every nerve in her body was reacting oddly to his presence and his nearness.

'You know, Olivia, I have a lot to thank you for,' he said at length, and she raised startled grey eyes to his. 'Frances has been a much happier and contented child lately.'

A peculiar desire to lash out at him took possession of her. 'Doesn't it trouble you to think that your daughter spends so much time in the company of an alien in your community?'

His jaw hardened. 'Haven't I been forgiven yet for the things I said that first day we met?'

'Yes, of course I've forgiven you, and it wasn't very nice of me to remind you of it,' she whispered, flushing with shame.

'What's the matter with me?' she wondered frantically as their eyes met and held for interminable, shattering seconds, while deep down inside of her something stirred, taking the shape of a warning she could not ignore, but was unable to understand.

'Olivia . . .'

He said her name in a way that sent a strange weakness surging through her veins and, leaping to her feet as if someone had fired a shot at her, she said hastily, 'Don't think me rude, Bernard, but it's late, and I—I have to be up early tomorrow.'

'What's wrong, Olivia?' he demanded, his cup clattering in the saucer as he placed it on the table. He towered over her suddenly, and the weakness threatened to overwhelm her. 'What's happened, since that day we flew to Johannesburg, to make you treat me with such cool politeness?'

She wrung her hands together nervously, wishing desperately that he would just go and leave her in peace to sort out these new and frightening emotions which we taking possession of her. 'I . . . don't know what you're talking about,' she evaded his question haltingly.

'Oh, yes, you do, and I demand an answer.'

He was beside her suddenly, his nearness sending a charge of electricity through her that made her tremble violently and clutch at the back of her chair for support.

'You're imagining things,' she said at last, despising herself for the shakiness of her voice.

'Am I imagining it that you're as jumpy as a nervous kitten whenever I'm about, that you've steadfastly refused all invitations to come out to Mountain View, and that you seldom smile these days except when you're with Frances?' His eyes raked her from head to foot, scorching her through the cool cotton frock. 'Am I imagining all that?'

'I've agreed to come out to the farm this Saturday, haven't I?'

'After initially refusing, yes,' he agreed with a cynical twist to his lips that made her wince inwardly. 'Do you dislike me so much, Olivia?'

Her hand tightened on the back of the chair. 'I don't dislike you.'

'Then what is it?'

'I—I can't explain,' she whispered hoarsely, frightened by the leaping flames in his eyes and the way the faint odour of his particular brand of shaving lotion attacked her senses which were now vitally alive and alarmingly receptive to his physical appeal.

'If you can't explain, then you must be confused about something,' he persisted harshly. 'Perhaps this will settle the matter for you.'

Her numbed brain flashed out a warning, but it came too late as she found herself crushed against the hardness of his muscular body, with his arms like steel clamps about her ribs, almost squeezing the breath from her lungs before his mouth settled upon hers with a demanding intensity that shook her physically and mentally as she fought against the darkness which threatened to envelop her. She was unable to think straight as she clutched at his arms and felt the muscles ripple beneath her hands, and then, to her horror, she began to tremble, her lips responding of their own volition to his lingering kiss, while her body, aflame with sensations she had never known before, relaxed against him. Her heart was racing at a suffocating pace, beating almost in unison with his, and leaving her devoid of any desire to be released from this well of exciting emotions into which she had been plunged. But she was set free as suddenly as he had taken her, and she stood swaying dazedly, clutching at the chair beside her while her breath came unevenly over parted lips that were still throbbing from the mastery of a kiss which had seared her to her very soul.

'Goodnight, Olivia,' she heard him say harshly as if from some distance, but ashamed and alarmed by what had happened, she could not raise her eyes to his, and moments later the front door slammed behind him with a force that rattled the windows and shattered the peaceful rose-scented night.

She heard his car being driven away, but she was shaking so much that she was afraid to move from where she stood for a moment. No man had ever kissed her in that way before. She should feel insulted and degraded, but she only felt deeply ashamed at the thought of her own ecstatic response. A sudden incredible anger gave her the necessary strength, and, scooping up the empty coffee cup, she took it through to the kitchen.

Bernard had had no right to kiss her in that brutal fashion, she thought furiously as she rinsed the cups and stacked them in the rack. Neither had she given him the right to force himself on her in that way, she told herself, tears blurring her vision as she dried the cups and saucers with more vigour than was necessary, and she had certainly not given him permission to continue kissing her until she had felt as if—as though—Oh, lord, *no*!

A cup crashed to the ground at her feet and, ashen-faced, she stared at the pieces scattered across the tiled floor with wide, feverish eyes. It *couldn't* be! Not Bernard King! Not *him*! He was detestable, insufferable, overpowering, and she hated him! But hate was not what she had felt when he had held her in those powerful arms of his, and hate was not what she was experiencing then as she relived those moments. She loved him; impossibly and irrevocably she was in love with a man she had feared, and still feared because of what he could do to her emotionally.

It was madness! she told herself, but her heavy, erratic heartbeats told her something else, and she dropped into the nearest chair with a moan on her lips as she faced the incredible truth. What would Ilona say if she should find out, and Tante Maria, and Vivien, and—Oh, God!—there was Frances too!

Heaven only knew what she was going to do. She had not *wanted* to love him. If she had had a choice she would much rather have fallen in love with Gerald, but certainly not with Bernard King whose brute strength she had been made aware of from their first encounter without him even touching her. No wonder her nerves had always reacted so violently whenever he was near, almost as if she had been subconsciously fighting against something she had been unable to put a name to, and now it had happened. It had taken only one brutal, lingering kiss, so typical of the man, to cause her neatly organised world to crumble about her, and to awaken her to the frightening reality of what he meant to her. Oh, lord, why did it have to be *him*?

The remainder of the week had loomed ahead of her like a dark, menacing cloud. She dreaded meeting Bernard again while she felt the way she did about him, but it seemed that he, too, had no wish to see her or speak to her, for it was Vivien who telephoned to say that Frances would not be coming to the shop that Saturday morning because Bernard would have no time to bring her to town.

No matter how much Olivia schemed and planned, there seemed to be no way she could wriggle out of going to the *braai*, but she finally pacified herself with the thought that she would be going with Gerald and Sanet, and that there would undoubtedly be several guests who would claim Bernard's attention. Whatever happened, she did not want to be alone with him. Not for one single minute.

It was almost five-thirty when she arrived at Mountain View that Saturday with Gerald and Sanet. Several cars had already been parked in the driveway, and the sound of laughter drew them towards the secluded area on the west side of the house. The sound of Gerald's car had apparently attracted Bernard's attention, for he appeared suddenly in the gap of the honeysuckle hedge to welcome them.

Olivia's treacherous heart leapt wildly, and the colour rose in her cheeks as she hung back, hoping to slip in as unobtrusively as possible, but, as Gerald and Sanet moved forward towards the guests reclining in garden chairs on the spacious lawn, a miniature whirlwind in the shape of Frances dashed past them and Olivia opened her arms automatically as the child flung herself into them.

'Olivia!' she cried chokingly, her arms clutching at Olivia as if she was afraid she would disappear.

'What is it, Frances?' she asked anxiously, pressing the smooth dark head against her, and forgetting momentarily that Bernard stood observing them with that brooding expression she had become so accustomed to.

'I was afraid you mightn't come,' Frances' muffled voice replied tremulously.

'We were both a little anxious,' Bernard added as her startled, questioning glance met his, and she knew instantly, and embarrassingly, that he was referring to their last encounter.

She lowered her eyes before his dark, disturbing gaze and loosened Frances' arms about her gently. 'Now that I'm here, Frances, will you take me to your Aunty Vivien so I can give her her birthday present?'

'She's in the kitchen supervising the salads,' Frances enlightened her, brightening instantly as she drew Olivia into the house and away from Bernard who stood watching them go. 'What did you get for her?'

Olivia pinched her cheek lightly and smiled. 'I think it'll be more exciting if you wait until she opens it, don't you?'

Frances nodded contentedly, and led the way into the large surprisingly modern kitchen where Vivien, with the help of the buxom, dark-skinned Evalina, was putting the finishing touches to an array of salads that was enough to quicken the appetite.

'Olivia!' she smiled warmly, glancing up from her task. 'We've had some dramatic doubts this afternoon about whether you'd come or not, but I'm pleased to see you're here after all.'

'Dear heaven!' Olivia thought distractedly, her cheeks flaming. Did Vivien know what had happened between Bernard and herself, or was she merely referring to Frances' innocent anxieties? Pulling herself together sharply, she kissed Vivien lightly on the cheek and pressed a package into her hands. 'Happy birthday, Vivien.'

'Oh, my dear, you shouldn't have,' Vivien whispered, obviously taken aback, but Frances could no longer control her curiosity as she bounced up and down beside Olivia.

'Open it, Aunty Viv, please!'

An amused but understanding smile flashed across Vivien's face as she obliged, removing the tissue paper to reveal the glittering evening purse with the delicately carved ivory handle.

'My dear!' Vivien gasped wide-eyed. 'Where on earth did you find this beautiful purse at such short notice?'

'I bought it originally for my aunt, but she died before I could give it to her, and I can't think of anyone else I'd rather give it to than yourself,' Olivia explained, aware of Frances' open-mouthed delight as she lightly fingered the small purse.

'I don't know what to say, Olivia,' said Vivien, a glimmer of unexpected tears in her eyes, 'except "thank you", and that sounds so inadequate.'

'It's so beautiful,' Frances crooned, sliding her fingers over the handle. 'Really beautiful.'

'What's so beautiful?' a deep voice asked directly behind Olivia, making her heart leap into her throat.

'This evening purse that Olivia's given Aunty Viv,' Frances elaborated excitedly. 'Isn't it beautiful, Daddy?'

'Beautiful,' he murmured, but Olivia had the uncomfortable feeling that he was looking down at her and not at the purse at all when she felt her nerve ends vibrate at his nearness. 'I think it's time you went out and welcomed your guests, Vivien.'

'Yes,' Vivien nodded absently, glancing down the length of the table and back. 'Oh, I hope I've done everything now.'

'Of course you have,' Bernard insisted forcefully, giving

her a gentle push towards the outer door. 'Now go out there and mingle.'

'I haven't seen Peter yet,' Olivia remarked nervously when she found herself alone with him and Frances.

'He was called out at the last minute, but he should be here shortly,' Bernard told her, taking her arm and sending a current of electricity through her as he guided her from the kitchen. 'Come through to the verandah and I'll get you something to drink.'

'Can I have something to drink too, Daddy?' Frances chipped in, and Bernard glanced at her over his shoulder.

'If you ask Evalina very nicely, she'll give you some of that ginger beer she's made.'

'Oh, goody!' Frances said excitedly, flying back into the kitchen. 'Evalina ...' Olivia heard her say, but the rest of her sentence escaped Olivia as Bernard led her away.

'Thank you for not disappointing Frances and Vivien,' he said finally, placing a glass of sherry between her fingers.

'You don't have to thank me,' she replied, her pulses fluttering nervously as he drew nearer to her.

'Are you still angry with me?'

The closeness of his tall, muscular body attacked her senses and sent a now familiar weakness surging into her limbs. She wanted to strike out at him, call him all the names under the sun she could think of, but nothing rose to her lips except a polite denial. 'I'm not angry with you, I——'

She broke off sharply as the gauze door swung open and, as they turned to face Ilona Haskins, Olivia could have sworn that she heard Bernard mutter an angry oath beneath his breath.

'Bernard, my dear, I've been looking everywhere for you.' Ilona's voice held a hint of a rebuke, her eyes disinterested yet watchful as she acknowledged Olivia's presence with a slight inclination of her immaculately styled red head.

'Would you like something to drink, Ilona?' Bernard asked calmly.

'Please, my dear,' she murmured, closing the distance between them and placing a slender, manicured hand on his arm with a possessiveness that made Olivia feel slightly sick. 'The usual, of course.'

In the fast gathering dusk Olivia saw Bernard smile down at Ilona with a certain warmth she herself had never seen, and her throat tightened mercilessly as she edged towards the door and mumbled, 'If you'll excuse me, please.'

'Don't look so agitated,' Gerald teased when she reached his side moments later.

'I'm not agitated,' she argued with an anger that was directed mainly at herself as she looked about her. 'Where's Sanet?'

Gerald gestured with the hand that held the can of beer. 'Over there talking to Vivien O'Brien and a collection of mothers whose children happen to be in her class.'

Olivia's eyes followed the direction he was pointing in and, as she glimpsed Sanet's gently glowing features among those of the other women, she turned back to Gerald and said: 'Don't neglect her this evening, will you?'

'I don't intend to,' he smiled, not taking his eyes of Sanet. 'There's something indefinably different about her this evening, don't you think?'

'Perhaps you're just seeing her for the first time in a different light,' Olivia replied absently, her glance going involuntarily towards the verandah where Bernard and Ilona stood close together, apparently engrossed in conversation.

Something hard and painful lodged itself in her chest as she dragged her anguished glance away to stare down into the crimson liquid as she raised it to her lips with a trembling hand. If to love someone meant one had to suffer agonies of mind and heart, then it was better not to love at all, she told herself, and to love Bernard King was certainly not what she had wanted. This love had been thrust upon her in the most unexpected manner, suddenly and forcefully, and she hated herself for letting it happen.

The fires were lit as darkness fell and the pungent smell of wood burning permeated the air as coloured lights were switched on in the trees to illuminate the enclosed area. Olivia found herself mingling somehow with the other guests, and she guessed roughly that there could be thirty or more. A number of them she knew by name, but others were no more than familiar faces she had become accustomed to seeing in her shop. With Frances at her side most of the time, as well as Gerald and Sanet, Olivia began to relax and enjoy the evening, and later, when it came to roasting the meat over the open fires, the men took over, leaving the women to gossip. The subject most discussed was the Show in January, and the articles which would be entered. Bernard, she gathered, always entered his cattle, and sold most of them at the cattle auction afterwards, which was something everyone insisted she should attend.

Considering that this was cattle country, Olivia was surprised to discover eventually that they had a choice of beef and mutton when it came to helping themselves to the food. Bernard appeared at her side as she circled the table with her plate, and her heart hammered wildly in her breast as she felt his arm about her waist, his hand warm against her side.

'Stay close to me,' he murmured, lowering his head towards her, but a stout-looking farmer drew him into a serious conversation concerning cattle breeding, and Olivia escaped unobtrusively, retiring to a quiet spot to enjoy her food with Frances sitting on the grass beside her chair, a heaped plate on her lap.

'There's going to be dancing a little later,' Frances remarked eventually, and Olivia was still trying to hide her disbelief when two elderly men brought out their instruments, a guitar and piano accordion, and amid enthusiastic hand clapping, the tables were pushed aside and the music began.

Peter, who had arrived some time earlier, swept Vivien

into his arms and started the dance, then others followed suit as the bouncing melody set everyone's feet tapping. Olivia did not lack partners, and almost fell into the arms of some of them when she happened to see Bernard approaching her. She did not want him to touch her, and dancing with him would merely remind her painfully of the few moments of shattering intimacy they had shared earlier that week.

A rugged-looking farmer with a sunburnt face claimed Olivia for the third time since the dancing had started, but a large hand came down on his shoulder in a firm but friendly manner, and held him back.

'It's my turn, I think,' Bernard smiled mockingly down into her startled eyes, but the next instant she was drawn into his arms and found herself matching her steps to his across the smooth lawn. 'Are you enjoying yourself?' he asked eventually, lowering his head towards hers in a way that heightened her colour.

'Yes, thank you,' she managed, a breathless note in her voice as she strained against him.

'What's the matter?'

'You're holding me too tight,' she gasped, her heart hammering so wildly against her ribs that she felt sure he must be able to feel it.

'I'm sorry,' he apologised, instantly relaxing his arm about her slender waist, 'but if I'm holding you too tight, then it's because I have no intention of letting you slip away from me again.'

'What do you mean?' she demanded, looking no higher than the top button of his V-necked safari jacket where a smattering of rough, dark hair was clearly visible on his tanned chest.

'Every time I've come near you this evening, you've darted away in the opposite direction,' he accused, his breath warm against her forehead and sending little shivers of delight through her.

'That's not true!'

'You know it is, so it's useless to argue,' he laughed briefly, drawing her closer to him so that their bodies touched, igniting a spark of unwanted emotion in Olivia. 'Don't disappear at the end of the evening, because I'm taking you home.'

'Gerald will——'

'Gerald is tied up quite nicely with Sanet Pretorius, and I don't somehow think you'll enjoy playing gooseberry,' he interrupted firmly.

A wave of helplessness swept over her, for she had forgotten how wrapped up in each other those two had become, but she would rather be an unwelcome third than have Bernard take her home, she decided. 'I don't think they would object——'

'I've already told him I'll be taking you home,' Bernard settled the matter, drawing her hard against him in order to avoid bumping into a couple dancing boisterously to the music, which seemed to go on endlessly before it came to an abrupt halt.

Olivia tried to free herself from Bernard's arm about her waist, and her cheeks flushed crimson as he laughed softly beneath his breath at her futile efforts to escape him.

'So there you are, Bernard.' Ilona's interruption had the desired effect, and Olivia was suddenly free as she faced this beautiful woman approaching them. She looked so casually elegant in her black slacks and black silk blouse with its wide sleeves that Olivia envied her, but the friendliness in Ilona's voice did not quite match the look in her eyes as they met Olivia's. 'Are you enjoying yourself this evening, Miss Logan?'

Aware that Bernard was observing her with equal interest, Olivia said brightly, 'Very much, thank you.'

In the cool night air Olivia caught a waft of Ilona's perfume as she turned towards Bernard and momentarily ignored Olivia. 'Be a dear, Bernard, and fetch me something to drink, please?'

He bowed slightly, his expression unfathomable as he glanced at Olivia. 'I won't be a moment.'

Olivia watched him walk away with long easy strides, the broad shoulders swaying slightly as he moved, and she bit back a sigh as she turned to make her way back to her chair, but a cool, slender hand touched her arm and detained her.

'It seems you didn't take me seriously, Miss Logan,' Ilona said coldly. 'Can't you see that Bernard is making a fool of you?'

'I don't know what you mean,' Olivia replied, holding her breath as she waited for an explanation.

'Come now, I've seen it all before,' Ilona laughed slightly, but the sound had a chilling effect on Olivia. 'Has he offered to take you home yet after the *braai*?'

'As a matter of fact, he has.'

'Then I'd take care if I were you.'

'What do you mean, take care?' Olivia demanded, instantly on her guard against this woman with the cold green eyes and cynical mouth. 'Just what are you insinuating this time?'

'I'm not insinuating anything, but don't lose your heart to him, because he's merely amusing himself with you, that's all,' Ilona added in a brittle voice.

That might have been all as far as Ilona was concerned, but it was quite enough for Olivia, who turned away feeling slightly sick with guilt at the hint of despair in Ilona's glance.

'Excuse me, please,' she muttered, and somehow made her way back to her chair before Bernard returned with Ilona's drink.

How much of what Ilona had said was the truth? she wondered as she sat down and felt Frances' hand slip into hers quite naturally. Ilona had lied to her once before, so why should she believe her now? Their six-year friendship she could not doubt, but had it ever been more than just friendship? Was there actually an intimate understanding between them, as Ilona had suggested?

Olivia was beginning to doubt this. Surely, if Bernard had been serious about Ilona, he would have married her years ago, and would not merely have been satisfied with keeping their relationship on such a platonic basis? But was it only platonic? Bernard was virile and very masculine, and Ilona was very beautiful. Surely they . . .?

Olivia literally shook herself free of this painful thought and, looking up, she met Bernard's eyes as he stood beside Ilona who clung possessively to his arm, with her head against his shoulder. With some distance separating them, Olivia could feel her skin tingle and her pulse quicken as she sustained that mocking glance, but she felt, too, the pangs of unaccustomed jealousy at seeing them together like that. It surprised her, however, and gave her an absurd thrill of pleasure when she eventually saw Bernard shrug off Ilona's hands and move across to where a group of men stood immersed in jovial, back-slapping conversation.

Beautiful as Ilona was, Bernard did not appear to want her, and hope fluttered ridiculously and guiltily in Olivia's breast despite the expression in Ilona's eyes as they met hers.

There was no longer any doubt in her mind that Ilona loved Bernard, and Olivia was beginning to suspect that Ilona, who had made herself unpleasant in the process of winning his love, was tasting the bitterness of defeat. It was a sobering thought, and one which awakened Olivia's sympathetic understanding. Ilona Haskins had been the target of unfair criticism for some time, but no one had ever stopped to consider that her behaviour might stem from an insecurity and a love which she must have realised was hopeless.

CHAPTER NINE

THE dancing continued till well after nine while the two gentlemen played tirelessly. Gerald and Sanet, Olivia noticed, seldom sat out a dance, moving slowly in time to the music and obviously totally engrossed in each other. Sanet looked happy, and Gerald? Olivia smiled to herself. Gerald, despite his protestations, seemed to have eyes for no one else.

Olivia caught a glimpse of Vivien gesturing that she wanted to see her and, leaving Frances to watch the dancing with wide, sleepy eyes, she made her way towards Vivien.

'I think everyone could do with a cup of strong coffee,' said Vivien. 'Would you care to lend a hand?'

Olivia nodded agreeably, grateful for the opportunity to do something useful, and followed Vivien across the lawn, but they had only gone a few paces when they came up against Ilona.

'Could I perhaps make the coffee, Vivien?'

'No, thank you, Ilona,' Vivien replied coolly. 'The coffee is made, and Olivia's going to help me pour.'

Ilona shrugged carelessly and turned away, but Olivia hesitated a moment, feeling desperately sorry for her as she watched her stroll aimlessly across the lawn amongst the guests. No one paid particular attention to her, and Olivia realised for the first time that Ilona was actually a very lonely woman.

'I wish I knew why Bernard invited Ilona,' Vivien remarked when Olivia caught up with her just outside the kitchen door. 'I can't stand her!' she added with a callousness that was unlike her.

'I think I feel very sorry for her,' Olivia admitted as they went inside to discover that Evaline had set out several trays loaded with cups and saucers.

'*Sorry* for her?' Vivien asked incredulously, her eyebrows flying upwards as she stared at Olivia.

'She's so insecure, and she's lonely, don't you see?'

'Ilona? Insecure and lonely?' Vivien echoed, almost choking on the words. 'Are you sure you're feeling well, Olivia?'

Olivia laughed a little self-consciously at Vivien's expression and, lifting the large coffee kettle off the stove where it had been left to brew, she began to fill the cups while Vivien poured milk into the jugs and filled the sugar bowls.

They fortunately did not have to walk far with the loaded trays before some of the men, Bernard included, relieved them of their task, and Olivia hoped Bernard would blame the hot kitchen for her flushed cheeks when his hands touched hers accidentally as he took the tray from her.

The musicians set aside their instruments to have a break, and everyone helped themselves to the steaming coffee. The mood was gay, but Olivia felt a little like an outsider as she observed the friendly familiarity among the guests. Beside her a dark head was beginning to droop with fatigue, and Olivia disposed of her empty cup before drawing Frances on to her lap.

'It's time you went to bed, Frances,' an authoritative voice spoke at Olivia's side before she had had time to persuade Frances to go inside.

'Oh, Daddy, must I?' Sleepy eyes blinked up at Bernard.

'It's way past your bedtime, young lady,' he pointed out, and Frances, unable to deny the fact that she was ready for bed, obeyed without further arguments.

'Will you come with me, Olivia, and stay for a while until I put out the light?'

Bernard frowned down at her. 'I don't think——'

'I'll go with her,' Olivia interrupted hastily, helping Frances to her feet and standing up as well. 'I don't mind at all.'

'Don't be long,' Bernard frowned down at them and, taking Frances by the hand, Olivia drew her towards the house.

Frances was so sleepy that Olivia had to help her undress and put on her pyjamas, and she guessed that, as there were no other children present at the *braai*, Bernard had given special permission for Frances to stay up late, and, no doubt, on condition that she remained inconspicuous. That would account for the child remaining quietly beside her chair all evening without making a nuisance of herself among the other guests. Olivia was almost certain that many of them had not even noticed that Frances had been there.

'I missed you in the shop this morning,' Olivia said as Frances sat on the edge of the bed removing the ribbons from her hair.

'Did you really?'

Frances raised her eager little face, and Olivia laughed a little self-consciously. 'Yes, really.'

'I love you so much, Olivia,' Frances said unexpectedly, drawing Olivia down on to the bed beside her and slipping her arms about her neck. 'I wish you were my mommy.'

Olivia's heart lurched violently and a lump rose in her throat making speech impossible for a few moments. 'That's the nicest thing anyone has ever said to me,' she whispered at last, hugging the child's warm body against her.

'You're crying,' Frances accused as she released her and noticed the tell-tale moistness in Olivia's eyes.

'No, I'm not, you darling scallywag,' Olivia denied with a shaky laugh as she picked up the pillow and threw it playfully at Frances.

Without a moment's hesitation, Frances threw the pillow back at Olivia with excited laughter bubbling over her rosy lips. Olivia retaliated once more, but Frances ducked expertly, and the pillow struck Bernard against the chest where he stood framed in the doorway.

'Oh, no!' Olivia moaned, raising her hand to her mouth in fright while Frances collapsed on the bed in a fit of giggles. How long had he been standing there? How much had he heard? Long enough to hear Frances' confession? she wondered frantically as she noticed his tight-lipped expression. He appeared to be waiting for her to say something, and her pulse was drumming so hard against her temples that she could think of nothing else to say, except, 'I'm sorry.'

He moved then, and came towards the bed to return the pillow to its proper place. 'The game is over. It's time you went to sleep, Frances.'

Frances' giggles subsided and she slid beneath the sheets with a meek, 'Yes, Daddy.'

His expression softened surprisingly as he bent over her and kissed her on the cheek. 'Goodnight, Frances.'

'Goodnight, Daddy,' she whispered, hugging him briefly and holding her arms out towards Olivia. 'Goodnight, Olivia.'

'Goodnight, darling,' she whispered, the endearment slipping out naturally and without her noticing as she kissed the soft cheek and hugged her once again. 'Sleep well.'

Bernard stood waiting at the door with an unfathomable expression on his rugged face as he stood aside for her to precede him, but in the dimly lit passage his hand closed about her arm.

'Stand still,' he ordered, and Olivia's heart raced as he turned her towards him. 'You've got a feather in your hair.'

Olivia remained perfectly still while he removed it, her senses sharpening at his nearness and the smell of wood smoke that clung to his clothes. She pulled a face as he tickled her unexpectedly beneath the nose with the small feather, and his soft laughter curved her own lips into a ready smile, but she was unprepared for the suddenness with which he swept her into his arms, kissing her roughly on her lips until they tingled responsively before he released her.

'Did you have to do that?' she asked breathlessly, struggling to control her wayward pulses as she looked up into his shadowed features and saw the hint of amusement lurking about those firm lips which had just kissed hers so thoroughly.

'No, but I don't regret it,' he replied, his glance suddenly mocking as he took her arm and sent a current of awareness through her that made her want to shrink from him as he led her towards the side verandah. 'Everyone is in a singing mood, and it's fun to join in,' he added as the sound of voices raised in song reached their ears.

Olivia glanced about her warily as they stepped outside, but there was no sign of Ilona as Bernard led her towards two vacant chairs. She was, however, conscious of several curious glances directed at Bernard and herself, but it was the look that passed between Peter and Vivien that succeeded in sending the blood rushing into her cheeks. She could imagine what they were thinking, but her wary heart was not ready to accept it yet.

They joined in with the singing of traditional songs, and she was surprised to find Bernard's deep baritone voice tone-perfect and pleasing on the ear. She tried to ignore his large, bulky frame beside her as the accordionist played the opening bars of 'Sarie Marais', but she almost leapt out of her skin when his hand found hers where it rested on the arm of her chair. She tried to free it, but couldn't and, afraid to look at him, she finally relinquished her efforts and left her hand in his large, warm clasp.

It was useless trying to sing after that, for no sound seemed to want to pass her lips as his caressing thumb against the back of her hand sent pleasurable sensations rippling through her body, and she almost hated him for being able to remain so unperturbed.

Gerald and Sanet were among the first guests to leave later that evening, and Olivia watched them drive away with mixed feelings. She had no option now but to remain until the last car had made its way down the driveway, leaving only Vivien, Peter, Bernard, and herself. Vivien organised the white-coated Venda houseboy, Abner, into clearing away the debris while Olivia succumbed to the request for a last cup of coffee before Peter and Vivien left.

'What about Frances?' she wanted to know, not liking the idea of leaving the child alone on the farm when they finally followed Peter's car down the drive.

'Evalina will remain in the house until I return, and so will Abner,' Bernard told her calmly. 'They're completely trustworthy.'

Satisfied, Olivia relaxed beside him, but her thoughts gave her no peace. What had happened to Ilona, and what had made her leave long before the *braai* had ended?

'Tired?' Bernard asked as the silence lengthened between them.

'A little,' she admitted, glancing at the dashboard clock and noticing to her surprise that it was after eleven.

'You could always put your head on my shoulder,' Bernard offered with a hint of amusement in his voice, and she instantly recoiled from the idea.

'I'm not that tired, thank you.'

His soft laughter made her blush profusely in the protective darkness, but he did not pursue the subject as he concentrated on the road ahead. As they reached the top of the slight rise, Louisville's street lights could be seen, and Olivia sighed inwardly with relief as Bernard's powerful Mercedes covered the distance in less than the usual time.

It was not the first time she had arrived home late at night and, as always, it gave her a strange feeling to drive through the small town with the houses in darkness, and the streets so quiet and deserted that one felt guilty about disturbing the peace.

Bernard escorted her up to her flat, taking the key from her to unlock the door and switch on the inside light, but her heartbeats quickened nervously when he followed her inside and closed the door behind him.

'Thank you for the lift, Bernard,' she said quickly, 'but I think you should get back to Frances, don't you?'

'Frances is quite safe, and I'm in no hurry.'

His softly spoken words gave her adequate warning, but her legs refused to obey her brain's frantic signals until it was too late for retreat. Fear and excitement clamoured for supremacy as she found herself draped helplessly across one hard, muscular arm, while with his free hand he found the nape of her neck and imprisoned her head as he lowered his lips to hers. She struggled feebly against him, but the warm sensuality of his mouth against hers sapped her strength and, for a time, she relaxed against his big, hard body, allowing the storm of her emotions to sweep over her until she trembled, her lips parting beneath his of their own volition.

This was madness! she thought fleetingly. Ilona had warned her to take care, but no one had warned her of the delight to her unawakened senses when the man you loved held you in his arms and kissed you with such passionate intensity as if he wished to draw your very soul through your yielding lips.

His fingers caressed her throat, lingering for a moment where a pulse raced furiously at the sweetness of his touch before he slipped his hand beneath the collar of her blouse to explore the creamy smoothness of her shoulder, and leaving a trail of fire against her skin in the process. Lost in the flood of her rising emotions, she clung to him, loving the feel of his hard shoulder muscles beneath her hands, and the strange fires that coursed through her veins at the gentleness of his touch, but sanity returned painfully as she felt his hand slide from her shoulder to her breast.

She struggled frantically against him, dragging her lips from his as she cried hoarsely, 'Let me go!'

'Stop struggling, you little idiot, you'll only hurt yourself,' he warned hoarsely, gripping her wrists as she thumped his broad, immovable chest with her fists, and twisting her arms behind her back to render her helpless.

'Please let me go, Bernard,' she begged, her breasts hurting against the hardness of his heaving chest. 'I'm not interested in a flirtation with you.'

'I'm not flirting with you, Olivia. At my age a man seldom does,' he said harshly, his eyes darkening with determination and anger as his grip on her wrists tightened painfully. 'I want you to marry me.'

'Oh, no!' she cried brokenly, realising now that he must have heard Frances' childish confession earlier that evening when she had put the child to bed, and coming to the painful conclusion that his unexpected proposal stemmed from nothing else but what he had heard. 'No, I can't.'

'What do you mean, no, you can't?' he demanded, a strange whiteness about his mouth while the leaping flames in his dark eyes seemed to devour her.

'Just what I said,' she replied unsteadily and close to tears. 'I don't want to—to marry you. I—I'm sorry.'

He was silent for some considerable time during which she was conscious only of his brooding eyes, and the heavy beat of her aching heart while she struggled to hold back her tears which were stinging her eyelids.

'I realise that I'm not a very good proposition for someone like yourself. A widower with a child seldom is,' he said at last, every word acting like the deliberate thrust of a sword to her heart. 'But I don't give up that easily, Olivia,' he added forcefully, his mouth hard against her own, bruising her lips in a kiss that was devoid of any tenderness.

An eternity seemed to pass before she was freed, and she staggered helplessly against the wall as he said 'goodnight' abruptly and left. Her breath rasped along her throat as she stared at the door which he had closed so firmly behind him, and then the tears came, hot, scalding tears that blinded her as she fumbled with the lock of the door and made her way to her room, stumbling over the edge of the carpet and falling on to her bed in a crumpled heap.

'Oh, God,' she prayed chokingly, pressing her tear-stained face into the pillow. 'He thinks I refused him because he's a widower with a child, but it wasn't that at all! He asked me to marry him for Frances' sake, but that's not enough. If I can't have his love, then I want no part of him, because I couldn't stand him to touch me if he was doing so merely because he considered it was expected of him. Oh, no, no!'

A fresh storm of weeping shook through her, leaving her exhausted when she finally had to undress and crawl into bed, but it had the effect of a sedative and, mercifully, she fell asleep almost instantly.

Vivien came to the shop just after ten on Monday morning and over a cup of tea Olivia questioned her about Ilona's early departure from the *braai* on Saturday evening.

'She said she had a headache,' Vivien explained with a thoughtful frown creasing her smooth brow. 'You know, Olivia, I've been thinking about what you said, and you were right. Ilona *must* be feeling very insecure as far as her relationship with Bernard is concerned. I mean ... she's been hanging around for six years, hoping, and I'm sure even expecting him to marry her. What kind of relationship they've had up till now, I couldn't say, but I do know that Bernard hasn't shown any interest in other women with Ilona always in the background. And Saturday evening, well ...' her expression was faintly rueful, 'I think everyone noticed the way he practically ignored Ilona.'

'That's why I feel so sorry for her,' Olivia elaborated cautiously as she stared down into her cup. 'She must feel quite desperate when she—when she considers she has competition.'

'Yes, one can feel sorry for her, but ...' Vivien hesitated, her glance mischievously intent, 'has she got competition?'

The tell-tale colour stole into Olivia's cheeks. 'I ... don't know what you mean.'

To Olivia's consternation Vivien laughed outright. 'Your blushes reveal far more than you're prepared to admit, but I saw the way you and Bernard were holding hands during the sing-song.'

'That didn't mean a thing.'

'I've never seen Bernard hold hands with a woman before, and certainly not with Ilona,' Vivien stated with a humorous grin.

'He must have held hands with his wife, surely,' Olivia remarked without thinking.

'With Aileen?' Vivien's eyebrows rose sharply in thoughtful surprise. 'I can't say I ever noticed, but ...' she hesitated, biting her lips as she came to a hasty decision. 'I'm going to tell you something I haven't even told Peter. Bernard and Aileen practically grew up together, and they somehow drifted into a marriage that was happy, but in a very dull sort of way. Aileen always reminded me of a completely unawakened young woman, and Bernard looked decidedly bored at times. Aileen's death was a terrible blow to him, of course, but I think his marriage had left him disillusioned.'

Olivia found that she had plenty to think about during the following two weeks, but much as she tried, she could not erase the memory of Bernard's unexpected proposal from her mind. That, as well as his apparent determination to stay away from her, made it all the more painful. He would drop Frances at the shop on a Saturday morning, and collect her again just after twelve without bothering to come in, displaying such complete indifference that she could only conclude that she had been correct in her assumption that he had merely asked her to marry him for Frances' sake. It was not a pleasant thought, and it haunted her to the extent that she cried herself to sleep most nights with his name on her lips.

Her framed tapestry arrived during this time, along with Vivien's, but there was no longer any joy in the prospect of hanging it against the wall in her lounge. It merely brought back painful memories of a day spent in Johannesburg with Bernard, and somehow she had to stop thinking of him.

During the last week in November Olivia received a visit from Gerald Thatcher, and she felt quite guilty at not having given him and Sanet a thought since Vivien's birthday.

'Where have you been hiding yourself these past weeks?' she teased him, and was surprised to see a flush stain his lean cheeks.

'I've been a little busy,' he explained, avoiding her glance. 'It's almost the end of the school term and there's so much to do.'

'And Sanet?' she questioned, guessing shrewdly that it was a little more than just school work which had kept him busy, and once again she saw his cheeks redden.

'That's what I actually came to tell you,' he said, his green glance meeting hers at last. 'Sanet and I are seriously thinking of marriage.'

'But how wonderful!' Olivia cried excitedly, but there was a flicker of envy in her heart as she drew his fair head down to hers and kissed him spontaneously on the lips. 'Gerald, I can't tell you how happy this has made me.'

'Good afternoon,' a deep voice made them draw apart swiftly, and Olivia's heart thudded heavily against her ribs as she saw Bernard approaching them with an expression that looked positively thunderous.

There was no doubt in her mind that he had witnessed that innocent kiss as she watched him greet Gerald rather stiffly, and Gerald, sending a hasty but curious glance in her direction, edged past Bernard.

'If you'll excuse me, I have a few things to do in town,' he muttered before hurrying outside.

'You can forget about Gerald Thatcher,' Bernard said tersely the moment they were alone, and something in his attitude reminded Olivia of their first, explosive encounter.

'I beg your pardon?' she demanded, determined not to be intimidated by him.

'You heard me,' he thundered at her, and she backed away from him involuntarily only to find the counter barring her way as he stepped towards her and towered over her in the most frightening way. 'Forget about Thatcher. You're going to belong to me, and no one else, so don't dish out too many of those kisses I witnessed when I arrived.'

'For your information,' she began, swallowing nervously, 'Gerald came to tell me that he and Sanet were thinking getting married, and that's why I kissed him. And as for the rest,' she drew a quivering breath, 'I don't belong to you, and never will, so you have no right to——'

A large hand closed about her throat and her eyes widened with alarm as she stared up into his mutinous eyes and wondered whether he intended throttling her. 'Say another word and I'll kiss you in a far more satisfactory way than the peck on the lips I saw you and Gerald exchanging a few minutes ago.'

'You're an insufferable brute!' she accused angrily the moment he released her.

'I know,' he smiled unexpectedly, and the aura of sensual masculinity about him filled her with a weakness she was beginning to despise as he added, 'But you will also find me a very gentle brute.'

'I'm not interested.'

'Given time you *will* be.'

His arrogance was infuriating and, clenching her hands at her sides, she pleaded, 'I wish you'd go.'

'But I've only just arrived,' he insisted calmly.

'You've overstayed your welcome.'

Angry fires leapt into his eyes, and the fragile bones in her wrist were in danger of snapping in his fierce grip as he jerked her up against him. 'No one speaks to me in that way and gets away with it.'

'Yes, I know,' she cried, tears of anger and pain filling her eyes. 'The Cattle King is almost a god in this community, but as I'm an alien you shouldn't expect me to grovel in the dust at your feet like the rest of your subjects.'

'That's enough!' he thundered, shaking her as if he wanted to do her a far more serious injury. 'What the devil do you think I am?'

'A bully, judging by the way you're hurting me,' she accused, fighting back the tears, and his grip slackened instantly.

He stared at her for several harrowing seconds before she saw his expression relax, and the twisted little smile that hovered about his mouth did odd things to her hungry heart.

'For a gentle little thing you have tremendous spirit, Olivia, and I must admit that you've not only captured my interest, but my admiration as well. Be warned, though, my dear,' he murmured softly, his eyes burning into hers as he raised her wrists alternately and placed his lips against the bruises left by his fingers, 'I shall take my revenge when the time is right, and it will be sweet, I promise you.'

Releasing her, he strode from the shop, but his forceful presence remained with her for some time afterwards. Olivia stared ruefully at the bruises that were clearly visible against her tender skin, but it was the touch of his lips against the bruises that still had the power to make her tremble.

Bernard did not come to the shop again, except on Saturday mornings when he brought Frances in to help her, but then he never came further than the door, and Olivia began to look upon his distant behaviour as a peculiar kind of punishment. She *wanted* to see him more often, and yet she knew that to be with him could only increase her unhappiness. He needed a mother for Frances, not a wife, and Frances had inadvertently made the choice for him. His proposal had meant nothing else, and she was not going to be fool enough to think that it did.

Two weeks before Christmas, Bernard strode into the shop a few minutes before she was about to close for the evening, and her heart somersaulted in her breast at the sight of him. Frances, whose holidays had begun a few days earlier, had accompanied him, and she brushed past him without ceremony in her haste to reach Olivia's side.

'Olivia, we should like you to spend Christmas Eve and Christmas Day out at the farm with us,' Bernard stated the reason for his visit at once, and Olivia stiffened automatically, wild thoughts leaping through her wary mind.

'You—you mean stay overnight?'

'Vivien and Peter will be there as well,' he added, the faintly mocking smile that twisted his lips sending the colour surging furiously into her pale cheeks.

'I . . . don't know.'

'Please, Olivia,' Frances spoke for the first time. 'Christmas won't be any fun without you. Please say you'll come?'

She had no resistance against Frances' pleas, but she suspected that Bernard was well aware of this fact, and was deliberately using Frances to strengthen his invitation. 'If it's important to you that I should be there . . .' she relented despite her convictions.

'You've just *got* to be there,' Frances insisted with an eagerness that warmed her cautious heart. 'Will you?'

'You know——' Olivia halted abruptly and flashed an angry glance at Bernard who stood observing them with a self-satisfied look on his face. 'You *both* know that I can't refuse you, Frances,' she added, dragging her glance from his as Frances grabbed her about the waist and hugged her enthusiastically.

'Yippee!' she shouted, her eyes dancing with happiness. 'Olivia, I just love you for saying yes, and so does Daddy. Don't you, Daddy?'

There was an awkward, heart-stopping silence before he nodded briefly, 'Of course.'

Frances talked excitedly about the preparations for Christmas, quite unaware of the strange tension which had arisen between Bernard and Olivia because of her casual remark.

'Yes, well . . .' Olivia interrupted Frances' animated chatter, 'it's time I closed up shop.'

'And it's time we went home,' Bernard remarked instantly, taking Frances' hand, but Olivia followed them to the door and watched them drive away, leaving her with a feeling of emptiness and longing.

The day before Christmas was scorchingly hot, and Olivia, despite the expensive air-conditioner she had had installed, found herself perspiring profusely. There was a suffocating humidity in the air which could only have resulted from the appearance of thunder clouds in the usually clear blue sky, but towards midday they piled up thickly, promising the long-awaited rain everyone had been praying for. It was not surprising, therefore, that she arrived at Mountain View, later that afternoon, in pouring rain. It had been a nerve-racking drive. The Apache's wipers were quite ineffectual in their efforts to clear the windscreen, and twice her car had skidded on the muddy road while the lightning and thunder followed hard on each other's heels with frightening repetition.

Bernard had apparently been awaiting her arrival, for she had barely parked her car when she saw him coming towards her with long, quick strides. He pressed an umbrella into her hands while he took her overnight bag off the back seat and, placing an arm about her waist, he practically lifted her off her feet in his effort to get her as quickly as possible beneath the sheltered verandah.

The smell of the damp earth mingled with the clean odour of Bernard's heated body and, for a moment, she could not decide which was the most dangerous—the electrifying storm, or Bernard's big, hard body against her own as he kept his arm about her and gazed anxiously down into her grey eyes.

'Are you all right?'

'Now, yes,' she laughed unsteadily, disengaging herself and glancing down at her slacks that were damp from the knees down.

'Was the road bad?'

There was a strange tightness about his eyes and mouth that made her refrain from telling him of the difficulties she had encountered, but a thrill of pleasure went through her at his obvious concern. 'It wasn't impassable,' she evaded his question just as Frances stormed out on to the verandah to greet her with that display of enthusiasm she was beginning to know so well.

Vivien and Peter were already there, she discovered when they went inside, and Vivien hastily showed Olivia to her room so that she could change out of her wet slacks before she joined them for coffee in the living-room with its comfortably padded armchairs and sofa, and wide glass doors leading out on to the verandah.

Beside the expensive hi-fi set with its multitude of dials and knobs stood a Christmas tree which was decorated with colourful baubles and silver tinsel, and after dinner that evening the lights which were threaded through it so carefully would be switched on in preparation for the exchanging of presents.

Olivia had found no difficulty in selecting a present for Frances, and had bought her a book which she knew the child had wanted for some time. For Vivien she had chosen an expensive silk scarf, and for Peter a set of fine linen handkerchiefs with his initials embroidered in the one corner. Bernard had presented a problem, though. He did not smoke, and she had no idea what his taste in ties was, for he seldom wore anything other than his khaki drill trousers and jacket or safari suits in that sub-tropical climate. She was close to desperation when Frances revealed that he was a keen photographer and that he needed a tripod for his camera. That settled the matter of a gift for Bernard as far as Olivia was concerned.

'These storms fortunately don't last too long,' Peter told her calmly as she flinched involuntarily when a flash of lightning ripped through the sky with a force that made her surface rapidly from her thoughts. 'You should be used to this kind of weather after living in Johannesburg for so many years.'

Olivia smiled wanly. 'The storms on the Reef are electrifying, but I don't think I've ever lived through a storm such as this.'

'You'll get used to it in time,' Bernard assured her, offering her a rusk to dunk in her coffee. 'I'm afraid, though, that our trip out to the baobab tomorrow morning will have to be cancelled. The veld will take some time to dry out after this deluge of rain, and it isn't much fun picnicking in the mud.'

Frances voiced her disappointment loudly, but she was old enough to understand and accept the wisdom of her father's decision.

'When Bernard and I were children, we used to go out to the baobab for a picnic with our parents,' Vivien told Olivia with a reminiscent smile. 'If you ever go out there again, take a look and you'll see where Bernard carved out his initials and mine on one such a picnic.'

'That was many years ago,' Bernard reminded Vivien with a smile that softened his rugged features.

'I know,' she agreed. 'You couldn't have been older than twelve, and I was then about six.'

'I bet she was a little brat at that age, Bernard,' Peter remarked teasingly, and Bernard agreed with solemn amusement.

'It's a pity I didn't know you as a little boy, Peter,' Vivien retorted with mock dignity. 'I'm sure you were the naughtiest little horror in the entire school!'

Bantering remarks flew back and forth between them and, after her ordeal on the way to Mountain View, Olivia found herself relaxing, and actually enjoying herself despite her misgivings during the past few days.

The storm subsided abruptly just before dinner that evening, leaving the air cool, fresh, and scented with the headiness of gardenias. No one dressed elaborately for dinner, and the atmosphere remained relaxed and informal, with Peter in an exceptionally witty mood. Lean and fair, and not exactly handsome, he possessed a certain measure of charm which, no doubt, had captivated Vivien initially, and a warm sincerity that awakened one's instinctive trust in him as a doctor and as a person.

'When are we going to hand out the presents?' Frances asked impatiently, obviously finding it difficult to curb her curiosity about the gaily wrapped parcels which had been placed beneath the tree before dinner, and finding it impossible to understand how they could still linger over their coffee when such an important ceremony awaited them in the living-room. 'It's after eight o'clock already,' she added, tightening her lips in a reproving manner, and resembling Bernard in a heart-wrenching way.

'I suppose we can't put it off much longer,' Bernard sighed resignedly. 'Drink up, everyone, and let's not keep this young lady in suspense much longer.'

The lights in the tree were switched on, and Peter was unanimously elected to hand out the presents, while Olivia somehow found herself seated on the sofa between Bernard and Frances. It was a devastating situation, for she was persistently aware of his muscular thigh touching hers and sending shivers of pleasure through her which she found difficult to ignore.

Peter supplied the humour while the gifts were handed out, speculating about the contents until he had everyone

fingering their wrapped presents, and making wild guesses
which evoked plenty of laughter. Olivia found no difficulty
in guessing that her gift from Peter and Vivien was a
bottle of perfume, for the expensive and subtle fragrance
had penetrated the wrapping quite tantalisingly, but, when
Bernard received *her* gift, several confusing suggestions
were made by everyone, and he was forced to unwrap it
eventually without guessing correctly.

His eyes flickered strangely as he stared at the tripod in
his hands, then, taking her hand in his, he raised it to his
lips and said quietly, 'Thank you, my dear.'

No one, fortunately, noticed her flustered appearance,
and within less than an hour the pile of Christmas presents
had disappeared, except for a small rectangular parcel
which was obviously the last, and most important of all,
judging by Frances' taut little face. Her dark eyes sparkled
with suppressed excitement as she relieved Peter of his
task and, to Olivia's utter astonishment, Frances turned
towards her and said:

'Here's another one for you, Olivia.'

'For me?' Olivia wanted to know, accepting it hesitantly.

'Yes,' Frances nodded quite firmly. 'Open it quickly.'

Surprised to find that her hands were shaking, Olivia
undid the wrapping while four pairs of eyes watched her
intently. Lifting the lid with care, she caught her breath
sharply, for against the wine-red velvet interior lay an expensive gold wristwatch, and the small card accompanying
it indicated that it was from Bernard *and* Frances.

Olivia stared at it with mixed emotions. She could not
accept such an outrageously expensive gift from Bernard
and his daughter, yet, if she refused it, Frances would be
deeply hurt. It was a devilish situation which left her very
little choice, and Bernard must have known this when he
had added Frances' name to the small card.

'Do you like it?' Frances asked excitedly, and with a certain amount of expectancy as she broke the lengthy silence in the room.

'It's beautiful,' Olivia sighed, expelling the air from her lungs as she stared at the intricate design. 'But I——'

'Daddy will put it on for you,' Frances interrupted her tentative refusal, and large, strong hands removed the small box from her trembling hands.

His fingers were pleasantly warm against her skin as he fastened the watch to her wrist, but Olivia found that she could not raise her glance to his. She had never owned a watch before, and she was close to tears at the thought that Bernard and Frances should have thought of it. He held her wrist a moment longer than was necessary, but as he released her, she turned instinctively towards Frances and hugged the child against her.

'Thank you very much, Frances,' she said in a shaky voice. 'I don't deserve such a wonderful gift, but thank you.'

'Aren't you going to kiss Daddy too?' Frances demanded happily after Olivia had kissed her warmly on the cheek before releasing her.

'Well, I——'

'Vivien and I promise not to look if that will make it easier for you,' Peter teased her mercilessly.

'That—won't be necessary,' Olivia managed, struggling to control the rapid throb of her pulses as she turned towards the silent man seated beside her. 'Thank you, Bernard.'

She raised her lips to his cheek, but he turned his head at the last moment and their lips met. She tried to draw back instantly, but his arm went firmly about her slim shoulders and, to her utter confusion and dismay, he continued to kiss her with lingering intent.

'*That*,' he stressed the word wickedly, 'was a pleasure.'

Furious and embarrassed, she knew only too well that he was referring to the kiss they had exchanged, and not to her murmured thanks, but Vivien and Peter, and Frances too, found the whole episode extremely amusing. There was nothing much she could do, she realised at length, except laugh off his kiss with flaming cheeks, but she dearly wished that she possessed the ability to wipe that mocking smile from his face.

CHAPTER TEN

OLIVIA was experiencing a Christmas Eve entirely different from what she had been used to. While her Aunt Georgina had been alive, they had always spent Christmas quietly at home, and usually alone. They had no family whom they could have invited over, and the few close friends Aunt Georgina possessed nearly always spent Christmas with their own families. Olivia's last Christmas in Johannesburg before coming to Louisville she had spent alone, making arrangements for her aunt's funeral, and Christmas Day had come and gone without her actually realising it. Now, as she sat basking in the warmth of this family she had come to know, she could not help thinking of the loneliness and despair she had lived through a year ago.

Shaking off her dismal thoughts, she tried to concentrate on the conversation, but Frances, who had been allowed to stay up late on this occasion, finally admitted that all the excitement had exhausted her and, saying goodnight to everyone, she went off to bed, clutching her presents against her as if they were her most treasured possessions.

With Frances no longer there, Olivia shifted her position on the sofa while Bernard poured them something to drink, but her action had not gone unnoticed as she had hoped. Vivien hid a smile as Olivia's glance met hers, but there was no mistaking the amusement lurking in her eyes, and Olivia looked away hastily, wishing that she did not blush so easily.

Bernard made no comment about the distance she had placed between them, and the incident passed without further embarrassment as they sat talking in the living-room with the festive atmosphere still lingering in the air. The hours slipped by unnoticed until Peter announced that it was after eleven and time he got a few hours' sleep before someone decided to call him out during the early hours of the morning. Vivien said goodnight reluctantly, following Peter from the room and, suddenly, Olivia was alone with Bernard.

'I think it's time I went to bed as well,' she said hastily, rising to her feet, but Bernard gripped her wrist lightly and drew her down beside him again.

'Stay and have a glass of sherry with me.'

'I've had one already, and I don't think I should have another,' she declined politely, but Bernard was already pouring the crimson liquid into two long-stemmed glasses and handing one to her in a way that made their fingers touch unavoidably, sparking off an awareness in Olivia that quickened her pulse.

'One more sherry won't harm you,' he smiled slightly, touching the rim of his glass to hers. 'To the future.'

An awkward silence settled between them as the tall, old-fashioned grandfather clock in the hall relentlessly ticked away the minutes towards midnight. Olivia drank her sherry a little too quickly, and it seemed to rush straight to her head, making her alarmingly lightheaded and strangely lethargic as she leaned back against the padded backrest of the sofa and fingered the gold strap of her watch where it lay warm against the delicately veined skin of her slender wrist.

'This watch was your idea, wasn't it, Bernard?' she asked, her voice sounding a little cool and distant.

'It was,' he admitted, turning towards her and cupping her chin in his hand as he raised her face to his. 'Don't you like it?'

'I like it very much,' she contradicted, his touch quickening her pulse, 'but you knew I wouldn't accept such an expensive gift from you, so you involved Frances and made it impossible for me to refuse it without hurting her feelings.'

'You're quite right,' he admitted, his eyes lingering for a moment on her soft mouth which was barely inches from his. For one frightening moment she thought he was going to kiss her, but he released her abruptly and moved a little away from her. 'Are you going to throw it back at me now that we are alone?'

He did not look at her, and she had a mad, impulsive desire to slide her hand over his dark, swiftly greying head to where the hair lay trimmed neatly against the back of his strong neck.

Alarmed by what she had contemplated, she said a little shakily, 'It would be most ungracious of me to throw your gift back at you, besides ...' she smiled then as he glanced at her with a curious expression flitting across his face, 'I've never owned anything as beautiful as this before, within a few minutes it will be Christmas Day, a day that shouldn't be marred by ill feelings or uncharitable behaviour.'

Bernard stared at her for some time, his eyes probing hers as if he wished to discover what lay beneath the surface of her composure before he drew her to her feet and walked with her in silence from the room, their footsteps echoing lightly on the tiled floor as they crossed the entrance hall, but muffled by the thick carpet as they turned off into the darkened passage towards her room.

Outside her door he drew her into his arms and sought the softness of her mouth with his. Lightheaded as a result of the sherry she had swallowed down too quickly, Olivia offered no resistance as he kissed her with persuasive warmth until she clung to him weakly, wishing that this moment would go on for ever, but, to her dismay, it ended all too soon. Bernard released her, and she swayed back against the door, staring up into his shadowed face almost accusingly as he stepped away from her.

'Merry Christmas, Olivia,' he murmured hoarsely, and then he was gone, leaving her confused and trembling with emotions which were becoming increasingly difficult to control.

Christmas Day was hot and humid, the air heavy with the scent of roses and honeysuckle as they lounged on the cool verandah. Evalina had prepared a feast for the midday dinner, and they all seemed to suffer from a lazy inertia afterwards, except Frances, who ran about outside catching butterflies in a miniature net.

'It's quite disgusting that she should be so energetic while I feel as though I've been pumped full of lead,' Vivien groaned beside Olivia.

'No one told you to eat enough for three,' Peter accused laughingly, following Bernard's example and leaning back in his chair with his long legs stretched out before him.

'I couldn't help it,' Vivien argued with a rueful grin. 'The roast turkey was just out of this world, and the plum pudding was superb. I just couldn't resist having a second helping of each.'

'I seem to remember that you had a second helping of several other dishes as well,' Peter continued, his blue eyes twinkling with humour as he counted on his fingers. 'There were the roast potatoes, the glazed carrots, the spicy stuffing Evalina had prepared for the turkey, and a liberal amount of cheese sauce on a double helping of cauliflower.'

'You're a beast!' Vivien scolded him, squirming a little as she shifted herself into a more comfortable position in her chair. 'If I have to rattle off a list of what you and Bernard consumed between you, you'd feel more than uncomfortable, you'd feel sick!'

'Then please don't,' Bernard groaned, touching his flat stomach gingerly. 'I don't think Peter and I could take it just at this moment.'

'But *I* was forced to listen to a résumé of all the things I ate,' Vivien protested indignantly.

'You're the one who complained,' Peter reminded her wickedly, grinning at Olivia who sat listening to this interchange in amused silence. 'I haven't heard you complaining yet, Olivia.'

'I'd better not,' she laughed. 'I'm just as guilty of eating too much as the rest of you.'

'There speaks a wise woman,' Bernard sighed lazily, clasping his hands behind his head and closing his eyes against the glare of the sun.

Olivia observed him for a moment, watching the rhythmic rise and fall of his broad chest, and the firm mouth above the square determined jaw. Her treacherous thoughts recalled the touch of his lips the previous evening, and her pulse quickened at the memory of her own response. His eyelashes flickered and she looked away hastily, out across the sunlit garden with its spacious lawns and colourful borders where Frances continued to stalk the unsuspecting butterflies.

This was a Christmas she would always remember, and not even Ilona's arrival at Mountain View later that afternoon succeeded in spoiling it for her as she watched the beautiful, slim redhead succeed in claiming Bernard's attention to the exclusion of herself.

Olivia went to the late night church service on Old Year's Eve and spent a quiet New Year's Day with Oom Hennie and Tante Maria, but Louisville became a beehive of activity during the following week as the final preparations for the show got under way. It was to be held that first Saturday of the month, and all the shops would close at eleven-thirty on that morning to enable everyone to attend. Tante Maria would man the pancake stall, leaving Oom Hennie alone in the shop that morning, and Vivien, Olivia knew, would be helping with the curry and rice. Everyone was involved in this event to some extent, and the excitement swelled among the inhabitants almost to a fever pitch.

Vivien rushed into the shop just after eight-thirty on that eventful Saturday morning, and wasted no time in coming to the point.

'Olivia, about that tapestry of yours.'

'I'm not entering it,' Olivia said stubbornly.

'The judging doesn't start before ten this morning, and there's still time before the entries close at nine,' she insisted coaxingly.

'Vivien, please,' Olivia began despairingly, her eyes widening with alarm as Vivien marched determinedly behind the counter and took the bunch of keys off the hook. 'What are you doing?'

'Taking your keys and going up to your flat to collect your tapestry whether you give me permission or not,' Vivien stated firmly.

'But, Vivien——' Olivia protested helplessly, but as Vivien hurried from the shop she shrugged her slim shoulders resignedly and sighed, 'Oh, what's the use?'

'Here are your keys,' Vivien said a few minutes later when she re-entered the shop with the framed tapestry under her arm, dropping the bunch of keys unceremoniously on the counter. 'Come to the show grounds when you're finished here this morning, and I'll treat you to a curry and rice lunch, with pancakes and coffee to round off the meal.'

'All right, Vivien,' she nodded, her glance appealing, 'but I wish you wouldn't enter my tapestry in the show.'

'It's too good to remain hidden in your flat,' Vivien insisted smilingly, turning towards the entrance. ' 'Bye for now.'

The blue Fiat disappeared down the street a few seconds later and Olivia shook her head helplessly. Vivien, like Bernard, was not easily thwarted once she had made up her mind about something, but such determination nearly always succeeded in sapping Olivia's resistance, and leaving her without a will of her own. She would have to take care, or she might find herself completely dominated by

these people, although Vivien always meant it in the nicest
way, whereas Bernard ...? Well, she could not be too sure
about Bernard.

The morning dragged by with very few customers and
very little to do, which was to be expected when all the
activity was taking place in the large open space at the end
of the main street, with its enclosed brick buildings, stalls,
and cattle kraals, which were used to their fullest advantage
on this one most exciting day of the year.

From force of habit, Olivia glanced up at the electric
clock against the wall before she remembered that she had
a watch of her own, gleaming on her wrist as a reminder
of this Christmas just past. Ten minutes past eleven.
Another twenty minutes and she could lock the door for
the day and join the thronging crowds down the street,
she thought with a touch of impatience.

'Olivia!' her name was called excitedly, and she looked
up to see Frances storming into the shop, her cheeks
flushed, and her breath rasping over her lips as a result of
running all the way from the show ground, no doubt, Olivia
thought as she caught hold of the child. 'Olivia, you've
won!'

'Calm down, Frances,' Olivia urged, unable to grasp the
reason for such frantic excitement. 'What are you talking
about?'

'Your tapestry,' Frances explained, clapping her hands
and bounding up and down with her pigtails flying. 'It's
won first prize, and you must come at once!'

'Frances, you can't be serious,' she accused in disbelief.
'Not *my* tapestry, surely?'

'Yes, yes! Oh, *do* come, Olivia,' the child insisted, her
face alight with excitement.

'I can't close up the shop,' Olivia dithered, unable to
believe the news Frances had imparted to her. 'It isn't
eleven-thirty yet.'

Frances was losing patience with her and grabbed her

hand. 'It's almost eleven-thirty, Olivia. Please come at once!'

'Oh, well, I suppose I might as well,' she agreed, grabbing her handbag and keys and following Frances quickly from the shop.

They drove up to the show grounds in the Apache, and Olivia found herself hovering between disbelief and a quivering excitement as she sought confirmation from Frances.

'You're not pulling my leg, are you, Frances? About my tapestry, I mean?'

'No!' Frances laughed, shaking her head firmly from side to side. 'I saw it myself, and Aunty Viv sent me to tell you about it, and to ask you to come. That's why I ran all the way.'

'I just can't believe it,' Olivia giggled nervously, unable to grasp the fact fully that her very first attempt at a tapestry should win the first prize in the Louisville show when there would be so many other entries from women who had more experience in that type of needlework.

'You'll have to believe it once you've seen the blue rosette fastened to the frame,' Frances said grandly, jumping from the car almost before it had stopped and grabbing hold of Olivia's hand. 'This way—quickly!'

'Not so fast, Frances,' Olivia begged as the child had her almost running through the crowds gathering at the various stalls.

'Olivia!' Tante Maria's voice called to her as they passed the pancake stall. 'Congratulations, my dear, with your tapestry.'

A smile flashed across Olivia's face, and pleasure welled within her as she faced the red-cheeked, blue-eyed woman, who stood flipping pancakes with a spotless apron tied about her plump waist.

'Thank you, Tante Maria, but I can't quite believe it yet.'

'Then go and take a look, child,' Tante Maria urged much to Frances' relief, for she promptly continued to drag Olivia in the direction of the large brick building at the other end of the stalls, but their progress was hampered once again when Vivien came towards them with a loaded tray in her hands.

'Olivia, isn't it exciting?' she wanted to know with a touch of arrogance in her smile. 'I told you your tapestry was beautiful, didn't I? You must go and have a look.'

'If people will stop getting in the way, then I might be able to get Olivia to the hall where her tapestry is so that she can see for herself,' Frances remarked pointedly in a very adult way.

'Oh, excuse me,' Vivien laughed, standing aside. 'See you later, Olivia.'

People were milling about admiring the entries in the various sections, but Frances took Olivia directly to where her tapestry was on display, the blue rosette with '1st Prize' printed in white in the centre proving, without doubt, what the judges had thought of her work.

It was unbelievable that what she had considered a paltry attempt at tapestry making should be so highly acclaimed, and she said as much to Frances who stood observing her reaction keenly.

'Don't go away,' Frances instructed after a few minutes. 'I'm going to fetch Daddy.'

Left alone, Olivia admired the other entries, and was terribly disappointed that Vivien's landscape had not won a prize. Ilona's tapestry of the Laughing Cavalier won second prize, and Olivia was admiring the fine stitches making up the face when Ilona's voice spoke directly behind her.

'I suppose I should congratulate you, considering that I've always taken the first prize in the past.'

Olivia turned slowly to face her, her expression carefully composed. 'I'm sorry about that, Ilona, but you don't have to congratulate me if you don't feel inclined to.'

Ilona's critical glance swept over the tapestry before returning to Olivia. 'I can't help wondering if you actually made it yourself.'

'I worked on it in the shop, and several people saw it before it was completed,' Olivia replied, startled by the hidden accusation in her remark. Did Ilona actually think she would have the audacity to enter someone else's work as her own?

Ilona's lips twisted cynically. 'Of course, if I'd had the opportunity to select my own frame, then my tapestry would undoubtedly have taken the first prize.'

Her barbed remarks were beginning to annoy as well as as inflict pain, taking from Olivia the joy of her achievement, and replacing it with a bitter regret that she had not been more firm with Vivien with regard to entering her work.

'I'm afraid, Ilona, I took Bernard's advice and left the selection of the type of frame to the people who did the actual framing, just as you must have done.'

'Why was your tapestry only entered late this morning?' Ilona demanded, obviously agitated at making no apparent headway with her accusations.

'I wasn't going to enter it, but Vivien came to the shop this morning and took it more or less without my permission,' Olivia explained quietly, her eyes mirroring regret. 'I'm terribly sorry, Ilona. I didn't intend to enter my tapestry, and I had no real interest in competing with anyone, so I really am sorry your tapestry didn't take the first prize. Please believe me,' she added, hoping to soothe Ilona, but something in her manner made the blood recede from Olivia's cheeks.

'I'm afraid I've underestimated you, Olivia,' she said, her eyes dark and stormy as she lodged her desperate attack. 'You've made an utter fool of yourself by chasing Bernard in the most shameless way, using your wiles on Vivien and an innocent child like Frances in your efforts to get what you want, and I wouldn't be surprised if you didn't, in some way, use your influence with the judges as well.'

A slap in the face could not have had a more devastating effect on Olivia as she stood white-faced and trembling, and humiliatingly aware that Ilona's raised voice had caused curious glances to turn in their direction.

'I think you've said quite enough, Ilona,' Bernard spoke suddenly beside Olivia, and Ilona paled, her eyes widening with something close to fear as he continued. 'You know as well as I do that the judges are not from Louisville and were therefore quite impartial, so accept the fact that you were beaten quite fairly. And, with regard to your other accusation, I suggest you get your facts straight before you say anything further. *I* have been chasing *Olivia*, and not the other way round.'

Olivia was left in no doubt that Bernard had heard every incriminating word Ilona had flung at her, piling humiliation upön humiliation and making her wish she were dead as Ilona continued her attack despite the attention she was attracting.

'You're a fool, Bernard!' she accused fiercely, but there were tears in her eyes, and they were tears of defeat. 'Can't you see what she's aiming at? Can't you see she's been deceiving you all this time, pretending to be fond of Frances, and cultivating a friendship with Vivien with only one purpose in mind—to trap you into marriage?'

Olivia felt desperately sorry for Ilona, but this final insult struck deep and, not waiting to discover whether Bernard believed Ilona's despicable accusations, she choked back her tears and fled through the discreetly curious onlookers as she made her way towards the exit. She would have run right past Frances had the child not clutched at her skirt, halting her briefly.

'Olivia, where are you going?'

'I—I can't talk now,' she managed in an anguished

voice, no longer able to prevent the tears from spilling on to her pale cheeks. 'I m-must go.'

'Olivia!' Frances wailed anxiously, but Olivia shook off her detaining hand and took a short cut between the stalls to where she had parked her car.

Brushing the tears from her eyes with the back of her hand in a slightly childish fashion, she drove towards her flat and, not bothering to garage her car, she rushed upstairs and let herself into her flat. Only then did she give way to sobs that rose in her throat, her body shaking uncontrollably as she lay weeping on the sofa with her face buried in her arms, her tears flowing until she was emotionally spent. When she eventually went through to the bathroom to bathe her face she scarcely recognised her own reflection in the mirror, and stared for a moment at the puffiness of her red-rimmed eyes, the paleness of her thin cheeks, and the bruised look about her quivering mouth.

What did it matter what Bernard thought? she told herself fiercely. Just as long as Vivien and Frances did not believe Ilona's vile statements. But it did matter what Bernard thought, her heart objected violently. It mattered a great deal!

A shuddering sigh escaped her as she went through to the lounge to search for her powder compact in her handbag in order to repair some of the damage to her face, but she was too late. The outer door was flung open with a force that almost wrenched it from its hinges, and Bernard stood there, tall, broad, and so frighteningly masculine that her knees threatened to cave in beneath her at the sight of him.

'What are you doing here?' she asked in a shaky voice as he closed the door gently but firmly behind him and came towards her. 'Why aren't you at the show grounds? The cattle auction must have started by now, and——'

'The auction can go on without me this time. You're more important to me at the moment, Olivia,' he interrupted her with surprising calmness, but she continued to stare at him coldly and defensively.

'You've got your priorities a little mixed, haven't you?'

'Sit down, Olivia. I want to talk to you,' he said, taking her by the shoulders and pushing her gently on to the sofa before he seated himself beside her.

'We have nothing to discuss,' she argued stubbornly, 'and—I—don't think I could stand a post-mortem of—of the encounter with Ilona. I've had enough, and I've swallowed enough insults to last me a lifetime. I just want to be l-left alone,' she added, and to her horror she burst into tears.

A large white handkerchief was pushed into her hands and she wept into the expensive linen while Bernard sat quietly beside her, making no attempt to touch her, and letting her cry until the tears ceased of their own accord.

'I'm sorry,' she whispered unsteadily, wiping her eyes and blowing her nose. 'You can see now why you shouldn't have come here.'

'Ilona asked me to apologise to you for the things she said,' he told her quietly, taking the handkerchief from her and pocketing it. 'She's not really as bad as she seems, and I'm actually partially to blame for what happened.'

'W-What do you mean?'

'Well ...' Bernard pushed his fingers through his hair and for the first time since she had known him he looked embarrassed. 'I've known for some years that Ilona hoped I would ask her to marry me, but I couldn't marry her when I didn't love her, and I should have ended our friendship long ago. I just didn't have the heart to tell her she was wasting her time.'

Friendship, Olivia thought, her heart feeling considerably lighter. So it was only friendship between them and not an intimate understanding as Ilona had wished her to believe, but it all pointed to something she had known for some time.

'Despite everything, I can't help feeling desperately sorry for her. She really does love you in her way, so her behaviour was understandable, I suppose.'

'I know,' Bernard said a trifle impatiently as he captured her trembling hands in his, 'but it's not Ilona I want to discuss right at this moment. Olivia, I've asked you once before, but I'm going to ask you again now.'

'If you're going to ask me to marry you, then the answer is ... no!' she said jerkily, wrenching her hands from his and jumping to her feet. How could she, after what Ilona had said, accept any proposal from him?

'All right, I won't ask you, but there's something you should know,' he said, coming up behind her where she stood at the window staring down into the almost deserted street with unseeing eyes. His hands were warm against her shoulders and she trembled as he turned her about to face him. 'I love you.'

Olivia went a shade paler, her heartbeats grinding to a halt before continuing at a reckless speed while she searched his rugged face for some sign of his usual mockery, but, although she found none, she still refused to believe him. 'You're only saying so because you overheard what Frances said the night of the *braai* out at your farm.'

His heavy eyebrows rose sharply. 'What did Frances say?'

'You know very well what she said,' she accused, shrugging herself free of his disturbing touch and placing some distance between them. 'You must have stood outside her bedroom door for quite some time before you came in, and that was why you asked me to marry you that night when you brought me back here.'

His eyes flickered strangely, but there was a sincerity in his deep voice that held an undeniable ring of truth in it. 'I can't pretend I know what you're talking about, but I went to look for you when you stayed away so long. I heard Frances laughing from the other end of the passage, and had a pillow thrown at me when I walked into the room. What was it that I should have heard her say?'

'You—you mean you didn't eavesdrop on our conversation?' she asked finally, swallowing nervously.

Bernard shook his head decisively, thrusting his hands into his pockets. 'I think you'd better explain, don't you?'

'I can't!' she cried, her cheeks flaring as she shied away from having to admit the embarrassing truth, but the look of determination in his eyes made her realise that he would not give up until he knew, and she sighed tiredly. 'Oh, very well! She said that—that she loved me and wished— and wished I was her mother.'

'Did she, the little devil?' he grinned humorously after her halting confession, but he sobered almost instantly. 'And you thought I asked you to marry me on the strength of that?'

Olivia lowered her confused glance before the intensity of his gaze. 'What else was I to think?'

'Olivia, I've been exceedingly selfish these past few months, and have thought of no one but myself.' His long legs covered the distance separating them in a few strides, and she was forced to look up at him when his large hands framed her face with surprising gentleness. 'I know now that I went about it in completely the wrong way, but I love you, and I want you and need you for my own sake. *Not* because of Frances, and despite Vivien's enjoyable matchmaking,' he added with a gleam of wickedness in his eyes, but Olivia was determined not to give in without a struggle.

'You called me an alien,' she reminded him sharply, despite the happiness that flowed through her, leaving her frighteningly weak.

'Yes,' he admitted, fingering a silky auburn curl just below her ear before he slid his hands down her back and drew her against him, 'but an alien who's intrigued me since that evening you came out to see Frances when she was ill.' His eyes probed hers relentlessly. 'Am I wrong in thinking that you don't dislike me?'

'I don't dislike you at all.'

'Do you think you could care for me a little?'

The hint of uncertainty in his voice caused the final barrier to crumble as she whispered, 'I—I think I can do better than that.'

His chest heaved beneath her hands, and she could actually feel his heartbeats quicken as he asked in a voice that was vibrantly low, 'Are you by any chance trying to tell me that you love me, Olivia?'

'Yes,' she admitted weakly, choking back the tears resulting from several weeks of utter despair, and the aching joy of knowing that she was truly loved, for herself, and not merely because he needed a mother for Frances.

'Will you marry me?'

For several seconds she sustained his fiery glance, allowing him to see right into her heart, then she buried her face against him. 'Oh, Bernard,' she whispered brokenly, releasing the floodgates for the second time since his arrival, but on this occasion Bernard's arms tightened about her small, slim body while he comforted her in a soothing voice, murmuring words that healed the rawness inside her, and filled her with a trembling, ecstatic happiness she had never thought to experience.

'You haven't given me an answer yet, my darling,' he reminded her as he prised her tear-stained face out into the open.

'The answer couldn't be anything else but ... yes,' she smiled tremulously through her tears.

'Do you think you could cope with an insufferable brute for a husband?' he teased gently, brushing the tears from her cheeks with his lips.

'You did say you could also be a very gentle brute,' she whispered, experiencing his gentleness at that very moment as she inhaled the clean, male smell of him while he caressed her.

'So I did,' he replied, shaking with inward laughter before his lips found hers and parted them with a tenderness that swept through her like a flame as she reached up and pushed her fingers through his crisp, dark hair; something she had yearned to do for so long, but did not have the right to.

'Why did you shave your beard off, Bernard?' she asked at last when he gave her the opportunity to breathe freely again.

He smiled then, a warmth in his glance that she knew was only for her. 'Frances told me you didn't particularly like a beard, and I didn't want anything to spoil my chances with you.'

'Darling!' she laughed up at him, but the word ignited a flame of passion in his eyes that seared through her as he caught her close with a fierceness that was wholly satisfying.

'Say that again,' he demanded hoarsely.

'Darling ...' she repeated a little more soberly, her eyes wide and luminous in the face of the overwhelming emotions she realised she was capable of awakening in him. A shudder of desire went through him and, caught in the wake of it, she murmured urgently against his lips, 'Bernard, I love you.'

The chime of the door-bell at that moment was an unwelcome intrusion, and Bernard muttered a soft oath beneath his breath as he released her. 'I'll see who it is.'

With his arms no longer supporting her, Olivia subsided weakly into the nearest chair, her heart beating so fast that she had great difficulty in breathing properly as she heard Vivien's anxious voice say apologetically, 'I'm sorry if we're interrupting, Bernard, but Frances has been terribly upset, and——'

'Where's Olivia, Daddy?' Frances demanded impatiently, cutting across Vivien's explanation in her anxiety. 'Is she all right?'

'See for yourself,' said Bernard, standing aside for her to enter, and a little whirlwind flashed across the room to land heavily in Olivia's outstretched arms.

'Olivia!' she cried, her voice muffled against Olivia's breast. 'You sounded so angry, and—and you were crying.'

'I'm sorry, darling. I was being a little silly,' Olivia whispered apologetically as she comforted her. 'Do you forgive me?'

Frances nodded her head against her. 'Yes, of course, but what happened?'

'It's no longer important,' Olivia replied, dismissing the entire, distressing incident from her mind.

'I think, Frances, that we arrived at the wrong time,' Vivien remarked shrewdly from just inside the doorway as she took in Olivia's glowing features and the slight hint of impatience on Bernard's rugged face.

'Your timing was not at fault,' he corrected suprisingly, glancing across at Olivia in a way that stained her cheeks a delicate pink. 'I've asked Olivia to become my wife.'

Vivien's expression registered surprise and pleasure which was almost comical, but Frances was the first to rally. 'Olivia, are you? Will you marry Daddy?'

Olivia touched the shining head gently. 'Yes, if you don't mind having me for a stepmother.'

'Oh, there *is* magic in the baobab tree!' Frances rejoiced, tears chasing each other down her cheeks. 'Do you remember the day we made a wish?'

Olivia smiled. 'Yes, I remember it well.'

'I wished then that you'd marry Daddy,' Frances announced without embarrassment.

'Darling, did you really?'

'Cross my heart,' Frances nodded, and Olivia caught her close in a rush of warmth and kissed her.

'As a matter of interest, Olivia, what did *you* wish for

that day?' Bernard asked with a speculative grin on his face.

'You're not going to believe this,' Olivia laughed self-consciously as she glanced up at Bernard and Vivien who stood waiting expectantly for her reply. 'I wished that Frances' wish would come true.'

There was a moment of absolute silence while they digested her statement, then a burst of laughter followed as they realised the significance of her wish.

'May I say how very happy I am for both of you,' Vivien said eventually, controlling her laughter as she embraced them both affectionately and enthusiastically. 'It's what I hoped for all along.'

'We realise that,' Bernard remarked, grinning wickedly across at Olivia who had gone through quite a few agonising situations because of Vivien's clever manoeuvring.

'Come along, Frances,' Vivien laughed, quite unabashed. 'Let's go and have something to eat. Your father and Olivia will join as a little later at the show grounds, I'm sure.'

Frances allowed herself to be led off quite happily knowing that Olivia would always be there in future and, as the door closed behind them, a peculiar little silence hovered in the lounge between Olivia and the man she loved so deeply.

'Bernard?' she questioned with a strange uncertainty as she saw a frown slowly caressing his brow.

'I know it's not going to be easy taking on a husband with a ready-made daughter, but——'

'I love you both very much,' she interrupted, banishing his doubts as she went swiftly into his outstretched arms.

'Where was I when we were so rudely interrupted?' he queried, sliding his exploring lips along the column of her neck and finding the vulnerable little spot behind her ear. Tremors of delight raced through her, and she pressed closer to him. 'Oh, yes,' he murmured huskily, 'I seem to remember that I was about to do this.'

His lips found hers, wreaking havoc with her emotions

as she clung to him unashamedly to do so. Passion flared between them as she melted into his embrace, her body yielding to the demand of his, and it was Bernard who finally released her with a groan on his lips.

'I think we'd better get back to the show grounds,' he smiled a little unsteadily, 'or I might not be responsible for my actions in a moment.'

Surfacing from her dreamy-eyed state of bliss, Olivia laughed softly as she drew his head down to hers and kissed him briefly on the lips before she left him alone for a moment and went through to her room to do something about her appearance. It was like a dream, she told her image in the mirror silently. An almost impossible dream that would most definitely come true despite all the doubts she had nurtured over the past months, and with Bernard, solid and dependable beside her, the dream would continue through all eternity. His heart belonged to her, as hers belonged to him. Always!

GIFT SELECTIONS

If you enjoyed our **Intimate Moments** gift selection, which contained four Romances not available before in paperback, you'll be interested to know that throughout the year Mills & Boon publish gift selections for special occasions, all containing four Mills & Boon Romances written by popular Mills & Boon authors.

LOOK OUT FOR . . .

The **Christmas Romance Pack** – available from October 1991.
Four wonderful Romances to warm your heart.

The **Mother's Day Selection** – available from February 1992.
Ideal as a gift or as a special treat for yourself.

The **Holiday Reading Pack** – available from May 1992.
Four Romances neatly packaged for you to take on your travels and escape from it all.

All our special packs are available from:
Boots, Martins, John Menzies, W.H. Smith, Woolworths and other paperback stockists.
Also from Mills and Boon Reader Service,
P.O. Box 236, Thornton Road, Croydon, Surrey CR9 3RU.

Mills & Boon

INTIMATE
MOMENTS

This Romance selection entitled 'INTIMATE MOMENTS' is a new selection we have introduced due to the large demand for our gift packs.

The special feature of 'INTIMATE MOMENTS' is that it contains four titles which we are publishing for the first time in paperback, the four titles have previously only been available in hardback.

As this is a new pack, we would like very much to know what you think about it, so please spend a few minutes completing the following questions, and in return we will send you a FREE Mills & Boon Romance as our thank you.

Don't forget to fill in your name and address, so that we know where to send your FREE book!

Please tick the appropriate box to indicate your answers ✔

1. From where did you obtain your 'INTIMATE MOMENTS' selection?

Mills & Boon Reader Service ☐

W.H. Smith, John Menzies, Other Newsagents ☐

Boots, Woolworths, Department Stores ☐

Supermarket ☐

Received as a gift ☐

Other (please specify): ―――――――――――

2. If the pack was a gift, who bought it for you?
―――――――――――――――――――――――――

3. If you bought the pack for yourself, what was your main reason for purchase?
―――――――――――――――――――――――――

4. What do you like most about the design of the pack?
―――――――――――――――――――――――――

5. What do you like least about the design of the pack?
―――――――――――――――――――――――――

6. **Would you like to make any other comments about 'INTIMATE MOMENTS' selection?** _____

7. **Have you previously bought or received any other Mills & Boon gift packs?**

Mother's Day Pack	☐	Holiday/Summer Reading Pack	☐
New Author Pack	☐	Mills & Boon	☐
Temptation Christmas Pack	☐	Romance Christmas Pack	

Other (please specify):_____

8. **How many Mills & Boon Romances do you read in a month?**

Less than one a month	☐	Five to ten a month	☐
One a month	☐	More than ten a month	☐
Two to four a month	☐		

Other (please specify):_____

9. **Which of the following series of romantic fiction do you read?**

Mills & Boon:		Silhouette:	
Romances	☐	Desire	☐
Best Sellers	☐	Sensation	☐
Temptation	☐	Special Edition	☐
Medical Romances	☐	Summer Sizzlers	☐
Collection	☐	**Zebra**	☐
Masquerade	☐	**Loveswept**	☐
Gift Packs	☐	None of these	☐

10. **Are you a Reader Service subscriber?**   Yes ☐   No ☐

11. **Are you working?**   Full-time ☐   Part-time ☐   Not working? ☐

12. **What is your age group?**
    16-24 ☐   25-34 ☐   35-44 ☐   45-54 ☐   55-64 ☐   65+ ☐

THANK YOU FOR YOUR HELP

Please send to: **Mills & Boon Survey,
P.O. Box 236, FREEPOST,
Croydon, Surrey CR9 3EL**

Ms/Mrs/Miss/Mr _____ IMOM 4

Address _____

_____

_____

_____ Postcode_____

mps
MAILING
PREFERENCE
SERVICE